IT'S MURDER, ON A GALAPAGOS CRUISE

AN AMATEUR FEMALE SLEUTH HISTORICAL COZY MYSTERY

P.C. JAMES

JAMES GANG PUBLISHING

NEWSLETTER

I hope you're enjoying the mysterious adventures of Miss Riddell. If you are, you may want to sign up for my absolutely FREE newsletter, which will keep you current on all things Miss Riddell.

1

TORONTO, CANADA. NOVEMBER 1988

'LONELINESS IS A CLOAK YOU WEAR.' That phrase from the old Sixties song kept running through Pauline Riddell's mind as she waited for her recently widowed sister Freda's plane to land. Freda had reminded her of the song on the phone only days ago when Pauline called to see how she was. It was true of both of them now but, Pauline thought, much more so for Freda. Freda and her husband, Keith Holman, had been that 'one person' the old church ceremony talked of and his death left Freda bereft. Her children were grown and gone. Really gone. In this new world, nobody lived nearby anymore. Freda's three children were scattered far from Yorkshire: one in London, one in America, and one in Australia.

Watching from the windows of the newly named Toronto Pearson International Airport, Pauline was relieved to finally see the Air Canada flight from London touching down. She began to walk to the arrivals area, musing on her own situation. She was alone but she didn't think she was lonely; she'd always been a self-sufficient person, even as a child. However, since moving to Toronto to take up an executive position with a Canadian company some eight years ago, she'd begun to realize the difficulties that being alone can bring. It was easy to shrug it off when she'd been younger but now, at age fifty-five, it felt like life was closing in on her.

That silly song was making her gloomy, she thought, giving herself a mental shake. It was typical of that awful period, a time when, in her mind, the societal illness that had begun growing in her fellow citizens in the Fifties had broken out into full-blown disease. Hedonism and decadence began in earnest during those years and hadn't subsided since. The Seventies had been worse, and the Eighties were unbelievably crass. She grinned. And somewhere along the way, while she wasn't watching, she'd become a cranky old woman. She rather liked that.

Freda appeared from the sliding doors and looked around. Pauline waved and caught her eye. With a beaming smile, Freda followed Pauline's gestures down the ramp to where they met in a firm hug.

"How was the flight?" Pauline asked, as she took control of one of Freda's cases and led the way to the parking lot elevators.

"Long," Freda said, "but everything was nice and, despite what people told me, I thought the meals were fine."

"And how is everyone at home?"

"They're good. They send their love and hope you'll come over again soon."

"It's expensive," Pauline said. "Maybe next year. All my vacation time and money this year is being spent with you on our Galapagos adventure."

"It will be an adventure, won't it?" Freda said, as they arrived at Pauline's car and began loading the bags into the trunk. "Did you ever imagine when we were growing up we'd ever be able to visit such places?"

"I didn't," Pauline said. "Jet travel is the most amazing improvement of our lives, I think."

"There have been so many," Freda said, "and yet I think

you may be right. Do you remember when Aunt Mabel went to the Canary Islands in the Fifties by boat and how far that seemed to us?"

"I'd forgotten," Pauline said, as she drove out of the parking lot and merged into the stream of traffic heading back to the city.

"I had as well," Freda said. "Then sometime on the flight, it came back to me and I realized it took her longer to get there than it was taking me to come here. The contrast just astounded me. Now, I can't stop thinking about it."

"Only sailors like Matt visited these out of the way places then, and real explorers like Jacque Cousteau," Pauline agreed. "Now we're visiting as tourists."

"And what I find even more amazing is I'm visiting Galapagos by way of Canada," Freda said. "It isn't so long ago people emigrated to Canada and hardly ever came back. The sea voyage took longer than the time they had for vacation."

"Now you fly here, meet me, and we fly to South America tomorrow. It's a huge change and in such a short time," Pauline said, edging her way through the busy afternoon traffic of Toronto's rush hour.

"How far is it to your apartment?" Freda asked, as the traffic finally ground to a halt.

"Not far in distance," Pauline said, "but it will be a while. Your flight landed at an awful time. It's the afternoon rush hour here."

"Oh. I never thought of Toronto having a rush hour," Freda said. "When you live in the country, you don't think of such things."

"Don't think about it. It's always busy here," Pauline said. "Think about flying out tomorrow to Ecuador and all the wonderful things we're going to see."

"I've thought of nothing else for days now so instead tell me about that case you've just been involved in," Freda said.

"I told you on the phone," Pauline said, unwilling to talk about her success.

"Why did you take the case?" Freda asked. "You always say you don't do sordid criminal stuff and a jewel robbery sounds exactly what you don't like."

"The robbery is what the media reported," Pauline said, "but there was a side to the investigation that was more than just one lot of greedy people robbing another lot of greedy people. It had to do with justice, which is something I do feel strongly about."

"Isn't theft a matter for justice?" Freda asked, puzzled.

"Of course," Pauline said, "when it's real people suffering. In this case, it was two groups who were fighting for control of something and hurting only each other. The police could have arrested either or both of them with equal justice being served."

"And somewhere in the mess was something you saw that was really wrong?" Freda asked.

Pauline nodded, as she pressed the gas pedal and rolled the car forward another short distance.

"A man died. Just an ordinary man who seemed to die in an accident. I couldn't let that pass. The law has to apply to everyone, including the rich, the powerful, and politicians, though so many of them are hard to catch."

"You're beginning to sound like your old colleague Chief Inspector Ramsay," Freda said, laughing.

"He said to me after one case that as I grew older I'd grow to see what he saw and have the same disdain for our masters that he had," Pauline said, "but I wasn't to forget that justice must apply to all and that means even the poor, no matter how much we may sympathize with their plight."

"What a strange thing for him to say."

"I thought so at the time because he was always so sarcastic when I suggested our leaders were generally doing their best. 'Our masters, you mean,' he'd say. But over the years I did notice he tried always to be even-handed, not favoring either side. I hope I shall always act that way as well."

"You're luckier than him, though, Polly," Freda said, reverting to her sister's childhood nickname. "You don't have to take cases where your conscience might be troubled."

Pauline nodded. "We're here," she said, turning her car into a side road and then down into the entrance to an underground garage. She leaned out and activated the door.

"I bet this is useful when the winter arrives," Freda said.

"It is. I leave my apartment in the morning, go down the elevator to the garage, get into my car and drive to work where I park in another underground garage before taking the elevator up to my office. I never have to feel cold or shuffle through snow or any of those things less fortunate people have to put up with."

"I'd miss the seasons and the way they make you feel," Freda said.

"Come back in January or August," Pauline said, smiling. "Not everywhere has seasons that are as kind as those in England."

Later that evening, as they sat quietly together in Pauline's apartment, Freda said, "If I lived here, I could become a coffee drinker. This is so mild. Not like the European coffee we got in Spain."

"The oodles of cream help a lot," Pauline said.

"Very luxurious," Freda agreed.

"It is, isn't it. So many things here are more affordable than at home," Pauline said. "I see why Mum and Dad always said things were better before the war."

"But you don't have a television," Freda said.

Pauline laughed. "Not because it's expensive," she said. "In fact, it's free here. No license fee to pay."

"I've just remembered; you didn't have a TV in England either."

"I didn't like it much then and over here it actually seems to be worse," Pauline said. "I'm happier with the radio and a book."

"I'd go mad without the telly," Freda said, "especially now."

"Which is why we're on our way to the Galapagos Islands."

"Exactly. There was this amazing documentary about them and Darwin only a few months ago. Then, when Keith died, and you suggested it, I decided I would visit them. After all, none of us know how long we have left, do we? We have to live for the day."

Pauline smiled. "I hope we both have lots of years left," she said, "and maybe lots more adventures together."

"It would be easier if you came home, Polly. You said it was only going to be for a few years. 'To see the world' was how you described it."

"I did indeed," Pauline said. "I'd always been a bit jealous of our dear brother, Matt, sailing around seeing the world while I sat at home going nowhere."

"Well, you've seen something of the world now so why not come home?"

"I did try," she said. "When I visited in 1985, I called and met with my old colleagues, but it was right after the 1984 recession and no one was hiring. You wouldn't know this Freddie," Pauline said, lapsing into her sister's childhood nickname, "because you work in the National Health Service, but Britain's industries have been wiped out. Joining the Common Market put an end to many of them and the oil crisis did the rest. The companies I worked for are gone."

"But the country is growing again now," Freda said. "It's on the news and everything."

"They're new businesses and not ones I have any experience in," Pauline said. "I'm afraid I just have to sit it out until retirement. Ugh! What an awful thing to say. Anyhow, only then can I consider where my future lies."

"You'll have forgotten us all by then," Freda said, sadly.

"Nonsense, Freddie. You're growing maudlin."

"I'm getting tired," Freda said, with a smile. "I don't know why sitting about in airports and planes for hours on end should be so exhausting but there it is. I shall turn in and be up hours too early in the morning."

"It will help you sleep on the flight tomorrow evening," Pauline said, "which isn't a bad strategy. I shall join you in early rising. Wake me when you get up."

Pauline sat quietly, waiting for Freda to finish in the bathroom. Having Freda here, and talking about Inspector Ramsay and family back home, brought back many buried feelings just as Freda losing Keith had brought back the pain she'd felt when Stephen had been killed in that pointless Korean War. And her pain was without being married for thirty-five years as Freda and Keith had been. Knowing something of how Freda felt should have helped her say the right things, do the right things, but it seemed her insides were numb.

In truth, Freda was here because Pauline didn't know the right things to say. Freda's chance remark, made months earlier, about wanting to see the Galapagos Islands had seemed like a lifeline to Pauline when she'd tried to console her sister. And it seemed to work. As the weeks passed, and they talked more about the possibility, Freda did recover her spirits until they'd made the decision and booked the trip.

2

TORONTO TO QUITO, ECUADOR

"WOW," Freda said, as she gazed through the plane's window at the towering peaks, some snow-capped, far below.

Pauline leaned across her sister to see what had caught Freda's attention. "Spectacular," she said. "I didn't know the Andes were so amazing."

"I didn't know anything about them at all," Freda said. "Now I want to visit them next."

"Hmm," Pauline said, amused. "Will Keith's life insurance stretch that far?"

Freda's expression changed immediately from awe to grief-stricken and Pauline inwardly cursed herself. Living alone did tend to make one insensitive to others as she'd noticed on more than one occasion.

She hugged her sister," Sorry," she said. "That was stupid of me."

Freda shook her head. "It's just too soon for joking about," she said.

"I do understand," Pauline said, "I'm just not very good at expressing it."

"You were never the empathetic one of the family, let's be

honest," Freda said. "Maybe that's why you're so good at what you do, at your work and in your investigating."

"Then like all things, it's a mixed blessing," Pauline agreed. "Now, in an hour or so, we'll be at the hotel and with luck we'll be able to see those snow-capped mountains from our balcony or maybe a terrace where they'll serve amazing South American coffees. Let's look forward to that."

3

ECUADOR AND GALAPAGOS ISLANDS, NOVEMBER 1988

THE FOLLOWING MORNING, early, the sisters were on a coach heading out of the city for the port of Guayaquil. Outside the bus window, a crowd watched a market stallholder whipping a young girl with his belt. Cursing and shrieking, the girl struggled wildly to escape the man's tight grip on her collar as the belt landed on her behind. Pauline Riddell watched dispassionately through the window, while her fellow passengers on the tour coach grew more and more angry.

Finally, a man unable to watch anymore, leapt from his seat and headed for the door. The tour guide promptly took up a station at the door to prevent him leaving before addressing the passengers.

"Ladies and gentlemen, *damas y caballeros*," the guide said, his accent becoming more pronounced as his agitation grew, "we cannot lose more time. We are very late, and this traffic will be like this until we reach the outskirts of the city. I understand what you see is very upsetting for you but please stay in your seats."

The man who wished to leave and rescue the child began shouting and other voices took up his demands for something to be done. The bus driver placed his hand firmly on the handle that opened the door to ensure it stayed shut. The driver's expression was thunderous; it had been from the outset when one passenger was fifteen minutes late and had then demanded to go back to the hotel because he thought he'd left his passport.

Pauline cursed that passenger. She could see him sitting at the front glowering at the driver and guide. Why he should be so angry with them when it was him who'd brought them all to this point of stagnation, she couldn't fathom. As she was pondering this inconsequential question, a woman in the seat across the aisle suddenly spoke to her.

"You seem unmoved by what we're witnessing," she said accusingly. "How can you as a woman, watch a child, a girl, be beaten by a grown man?"

"The spectators aren't unhappy and nor is the policeman I can see," Pauline said. "I presume the child tried to steal from the stall and was caught."

"But she's a child," the woman cried, growing even more red in the face.

"We don't let children steal; why would these people?"

"She was probably starving," the woman said. "It's barbaric."

"You don't know she is starving and it's only recently that corporal punishment of children ended in our countries," Pauline replied, hoping strict neutrality and a calm demeanor would lower passions all around.

"I've no doubt you'd be happy to whip them yourself, you callous creature."

"I'm sure the child knew the risks and the consequences of stealing," Pauline said. Outside, she saw the man had let go of the child and she was backing away, calling him names as she went.

"That policeman should have arrested that brute," the

woman said, slightly calmer now the incident was over and no longer inflaming her anger.

"Then what?" Pauline said. "He'd also arrest the girl for theft. She'd likely be put in a juvenile facility and lost to her family, as such children are in our own world. How is that better?"

The woman turned away in disgust, an angry retort clearly being held back.

"But Pauline it was horrible," Freda said. "Our parents didn't treat us that way. Even if we'd stolen something, they wouldn't have hit us like that."

"I'm not saying what we saw was nice," Pauline said, "only that it's clearly the way things are done here. After all, no one watching was objecting. Outsiders should be wary of interfering."

"That these people think it's okay doesn't make it right," the woman across the aisle cried, jumping into the conversation.

"The law or the native custom has to be followed. 'When in Rome, do as the Romans do' is good advice," Pauline said.

"Just because something is the law, doesn't make it right either," the woman said.

"Bad laws must be changed by society, not ignored by people who just don't like them," Pauline said. "That way lies chaos and eventually, violence."

The woman harrumphed and looked away again.

Freda said, "Thankfully, we're moving again."

She was right. Slowly the traffic was edging its way forward, carrying the bus with it. It was going to be a long trip down the highway to the cruise ship.

* * *

IT WAS INDEED a long journey and Pauline was not feeling any more charitable toward her fellow passengers, the Ecuadorean officials, the tour company's guide, or the world in general by the time they arrived. The drive down to Guayaquil from the airport hotel at Quito had been torturous. The road was rough and the coach's suspension hard. The traffic had made it uncomfortably long and also hot, for the coach's air-conditioning hadn't functioned well, if it had been working at all. She observed her fellow passengers without any of that goodwill vacations were supposed to engender, as they too waited in line to join the ship at Guayaquil's hastily erected, and clearly newly named, Cruise Ship Dock. Her fellow passengers, she observed, were the usual crowd of elderly couples, retired single men with large camera equipment packs, and women with overstuffed hand luggage, and a very small number of families. One man standing nearby with two plastic bags that clinked as he shuffled forward with the line looked as if he'd started partying the night before. She hoped her face didn't betray her silent prayer that he not be anywhere near her cabin.

"Polly, wake up!" Freda said, nudging her as she stepped forward. Pauline realized her focus on the passengers had caused her to miss the line moving again. She picked up her carry-on bag and walked two steps forward and put her bag down again. Like the coach, the line was not moving well.

Pauline returned to watching the passengers. One couple, who looked very young, belied their age by wearing sober, old-fashioned clothing and looking strangely traditional for such a youthful pair. The woman wore a headscarf as Mennonite and Amish folk do. Perhaps that's what they are, she thought, and moved on to survey the rest of the people in line. They weren't exactly the kind of people she'd seen on the previous cruises she'd been on. In the Caribbean, where her previous cruising had mainly been, people were flamboyantly dressed and bejeweled. This cruise group were a more outdoorsy set, with lots of khaki clothing and bush hats. Sensible enough for hiking across the bare terrain of the Galapagos Islands and yet strangely out of place in her experience of cruise ships. She hoped they weren't all naturalists who would only discuss iguanas and finches at every mealtime.

Like all waiting lines – fortunately this was a small ship because the Ecuadorian government was reducing the numbers who could be on the islands at any one time – this one eventually came to an end, and Pauline and Freda were sipping their welcome-aboard mimosas by late afternoon. Thirty minutes later, they were in their cabins next door to each other on Deck 3. The crossing from the mainland to the islands was to take a day and a half, and the voyage was organized for the guests to have dinner, socialize, and then miss most of the crossing time while sleeping.

Their bags arrived. They unpacked and freshened themselves before Pauline and Freda met outside their doors to begin exploring the ship. The moment they stepped outside their cabins, their cabin stewardess greeted them with a broad smile.

"Good afternoon, Señora Holman and Señorita Riddell. My name is Maria. I will be looking after your rooms during the voyage."

Maria was a petite woman, slim and hardly more than five feet tall, with black hair and dark eyes. "If you should need anything, just call me. My number is beside the phone in your cabin."

"Thank you, Maria," Freda said, peering at Maria's name badge. "You're from Peru, I see."

"Yes, madam, but I am very fortunate not to live there anymore." Maria's smile grew broader.

"From what I hear and read, you are indeed fortunate," Pauline said. "Where do you live now?"

"In Quito, Ecuador," Maria replied, "where I am among good people."

"Quito seemed a wonderful city," Pauline said. She saw Maria was already looking to move and introduce herself to a couple entering their room farther down the corridor. "I see others arriving," Pauline added. "You must go. We shall certainly call if we need something."

Maria hurried away to greet the couple before they disappeared into their cabin while the two sisters headed for the elevators. They'd agreed to watch the sail out before dining. Pauline had done three cruises, but for Freda this was the first time. As Pauline assured her, the sail out warranted standing outside in the fresh late afternoon breeze blowing in from the sea.

4

FIRST EVENING. AT SEA

AT DINNER, they were seated at a table with a collection of ill-assorted people: a morose, overweight single man named Arvin Weiss, who was the person responsible for holding them up that morning; the Mennonite couple Pauline had seen earlier, who were Ruth and Isaac Brandt; a young man from Toronto, Jason Somerville, who announced he was a police detective; and an oddly mismatched American couple, Rod and Betty Chalmers.

The mismatched couple were a revelation. Pauline had read of such pairings, especially in murder mysteries where contested wills were featured, but she had never met one in real life. Rod was in his thirties, but only just, Pauline guessed. Betty was in her seventies, maybe even older. She was a wealthy widow and he had been her exercise instructor, until a week ago. Now they were on their honeymoon, having the trip of a lifetime. She was loud and gay, the excited bride of fevered imagination; he was silent and only spoke in sarcastic rejoinders to anything, indeed everything, anyone said. Pauline hoped they'd find a different table for the rest of the cruise.

Arvin was an equally unsatisfactory dinner companion.

As with many overweight people, his clothes didn't fit, particularly around the middle, giving a general air of being down on his luck. His brown hair was thinning, combed over and straggling in so many opposite directions it looked as if he'd cut it himself. His sour expression took a turn for the worse when the Toronto detective said, "Your *forgotten* passport did us no favors, Arvin." The stress on 'forgotten' was warranted for Mr. Weiss had it in his pocket the whole time, as it turned out.

"I missed it, okay? So, what! The driver didn't need to make such a big deal out of it but I knew he would the moment I saw him. He's an Arab and hated me because he could see I was Jewish."

"Arvin," the whole table seemed to call out in unison, before the detective said, "The coach driver's name was Ernesto Lopez, it was on his badge and on the certificate above the windshield. He was Mexican and he was angry because you were fifteen minutes late to the coach and then you went back for the passport you thought you'd left in the hotel."

"What's it to him if he's late. I'm the paying passenger, he's the driver." Arvin's face grew quite pink in his agitation.

"The delay meant we'd missed the opportunity to avoid the rush hour traffic, which put the driver in considerable difficulty trying to catch up time on a busy road," Rod Chalmers growled.

Pauline thought he seemed equally as angry as the driver had been. Arvin, however, would have none of it and the squabble continued to burst out during the meal. Pauline sincerely hoped Arvin would find a different table for the rest of the voyage or even fall overboard on the first night. She hadn't enjoyed the coach trip either and for that too she blamed Arvin.

The detective, Jason, was eager and opinionated on every

topic that was discussed, not at all what people expected of Canadians. His fingers constantly thrummed the table in his apparent inability to be still. He spoke in the same way, bursting into conversations with blunt statements that brooked no opposition or discussion.

When Freda was unwise enough to tell the other guests she was from England, and Pauline now lived in Toronto, Somerville practically pounced.

"Where in Toronto," he demanded, in a voice Pauline was sure didn't bring out the best in anyone he was interrogating.

"High Park," Pauline said, "and you?"

"Oh, nowhere so grand," he replied. "Leaside. I grew up there. Do you know it?"

"I'm afraid I don't, Mr. Somerville," Pauline said. "I go out so little. The Eaton Centre, Yorkville and Hazelton Lanes are the limit of my exploring."

"Yorkville's great, isn't it?" Somerville said.

"You're a young man," Pauline said, "and would naturally enjoy it. I enjoy the liveliness but find the clothes don't suit me so much." She smiled to show she wasn't being too serious.

Realizing they were beginning to silence everyone else in this exchange, Pauline said, "I think you must be from Ontario as well, Mr. and Mrs. Brandt?"

The conversation moved on in desultory fashion and Pauline was very conscious of the young detective's regular speculative glances in her direction, as though trying to remember her. She was pleased when, after the dessert, he leapt out of his seat, declined the coffee and declared it time for a night cap, an oddly old-fashioned phrase for one so young. He headed straight for the bar at the end of the lounge where he joined a group of men loudly discussing football.

The Mennonite couple stayed on after the others had left and it gave Pauline an opportunity to learn more about this

Christian sect of which she knew so little. Few outside their communities in Canada and the USA did know much about them though there was plenty of speculation. Their formal manners and language pleased Pauline who'd found the world since the beginning of the Sixties a disappointing and disturbing place.

"If you don't mind me asking," Pauline said, "how do two Mennonite folks come to be outside their own world and aboard a ship of such unserious people?"

Isaac replied, "We're part of a reformed group who don't abjure all modern inventions or customs."

"You'll see plenty of new customs on the ship over the next ten days," Pauline said wryly. "I know I was shocked the first time I went on a cruise."

Ruth smiled. "Our mutual faith and support will help us survive the modern Western World," she said.

While Ruth was speaking, there was a definite smile in Isaac's eyes, though his expression remained neutral, and Pauline guessed they were gently teasing her, which in itself made them the best of their dinner companions of the evening.

After dinner, Freda and Pauline wrapped up warmly and walked the deck under the stars. It was surprising how cold the night air was at sea on the Equator. MS Orillia was an old ship of the sort Pauline had seen many times in harbors up and down England's east coast. The brochure said it had been built for the Far Eastern trade at the end of the Second World War but, when that trade never recovered, it had been converted to a cruise ship and sailed the Mediterranean until this last year when it had been refurbished to sail this remote part of the world. It almost smelled new, Pauline thought, or maybe that was the scent of the tropical sea that lay all around. Despite the Orillia's age, here under the Milky Way glowing in a great arc across the sky, and the almost full moon that cast a silver lane from horizon to ship, the ship looked ethereally beautiful in her newly painted white livery.

When she was sure nobody was about, Freda said quietly, "I do hope we get a different table for dinner tomorrow night."

Pauline laughed. "You too?" she said. "Really, I could murder that silly man Arvin."

"The other one, Rod, wasn't much better," Freda said. "He snapped at everything anyone said with such cutting, unpleasant comments."

"I wonder why Arvin even came?" Pauline said. "He says he can't stand the heat, felt too unwell to eat anything at dinner and wasn't sure he would ever be able to eat anything because it wasn't kosher. He had no discernible interest in evolution, Darwin, Ecuador or the islands. A strange way to spend the small fortune this cruise costs, I should think."

"I wish he hadn't come, or the other two," Freda said bluntly.

"And our Canadian detective?"

"I think he was just nervous. Did you see his fingers? They never stopped drumming on the table. I think he may have a had a drink or two before dinner," Freda said.

"It was probably the trip down here that upset them all," Pauline said. "I know I felt like death when we arrived. Maybe they'll perk up after a good night's sleep."

"They were setting out to fortify themselves with even more alcohol when we left so I expect they will sleep well," Freda replied. "I think I'm going to have a nap myself before we listen to the naturalist's talk. It has been a long day."

When they reached the exterior door that was nearest their cabins, Freda pulled it open and stepped inside. Pauline, however, stopped. Farther down the deck, in a place shadowed by lifeboats and the ship's superstructure, she saw a dark bundle that looked vaguely human-shaped.

"Pauline," Freda said, "are you coming?" She strained to hold open the heavy door.

"In a moment, Freddie," Pauline said. "There's something strange on the deck. I'll just go and investigate."

"What is it?" Freda asked, peering around the door and following Pauline's gaze.

"Probably one of the maintenance crew's bag or jacket but it may be a passenger who has fainted – or worse."

Pauline strode down the deck until she stood beside the man. She crouched and shook his shoulder. He didn't move so she took his wrist in her fingers. As she'd already suspected, though hoped she was wrong, he was dead. Not dead long for he was still 'alive' warm. She looked up. The decks above were lit but no one was in sight.

"What is it?" Freda called, repeating her question.

"It's a man. He's dead. Go and phone reception. Tell them there's been an accident on the starboard side, deck three, at the lifeboat station. I'll stay with the body until someone in authority comes."

Pauline saw the door close and hoped Freda would be quick. Why the man was dead, she couldn't yet say, but she knew not to touch the body until the police arrived. But there were no police, she thought, shaking her head. She checked his pulse again, this time at his neck, and felt the sickening looseness there. There was no question; it was broken. She rather hoped Freda would get back before the 'person in authority' because Freda was a principal nursing officer – what used to be called a matron before they'd foolishly allowed men into the profession. However, she was confident her own knowledge from the bodies she'd witnessed down the years of detecting, and her fingertips, were not deceiving her. He was dead. Then she saw blood on her fingers and peered carefully at his throat. His beard hid the wound but somewhere under his chin looked to be the reason for his death.

A light back along the deck told her Freda or crew members were arriving. She wished she'd had her camera with her. Pictures were useful things to have as memory aids later. She stood and surveyed the scene, hoping to fix it in her mind.

"They say someone will be here soon," Freda said, as she arrived at her sister's side. "I thought I should come and join you, in case…"

"In case it's murder and the murderer is still about," Pauline finished the sentence for her. "I think it is murder and I'd like your professional opinion before anyone gets here."

Freda crouched down and felt for a pulse. Not finding one, she felt the skin temperature.

"Look under his chin," Pauline said.

Freda tipped the head back and gingerly touched the bloodied hair of his beard. She knelt and looked more closely.

"He's been stabbed," she said.

"Yes. Then thrown, or maybe just fell, over one of the railings up there."

"He has a name tag," Freda said. "He's not one of the servers," she added.

Pauline nodded. "Jose, Peru," she said. As she spoke, a door opened and two men stepped out to greet them. One wore an officer's uniform, the other had a medicine bag. Pauline was unimpressed. He was the kind of doctor that failed to present himself as an example to the public. There had been some in her time, but they generally didn't stay long at any one place. She now knew where they went.

"Is he dead?" the officer asked Freda.

"Oh, yes. Quite dead," Freda replied.

"As the ship's doctor," the man with the bag said, "I'll be the one to confirm death."

Pauline couldn't decide if he was being ironic or was genuinely put out by Freda's assertion.

"You're certainly the one who must sign the certificate, Doctor," she said.

The doctor did all that was expected and pronounced Jose dead. He looked up. "Must have fallen from up there and broken his neck," he said.

"There's blood under his chin," Pauline said.

"Could have caught on a brace or stanchion," the doctor said, nodding. "We'll check for that when it's light."

"Can you tell us your names?" the officer asked. "They didn't tell us who found the body."

"I'm Pauline Riddell," Pauline replied, "and this is my sister, Mrs. Freda Holman. We're traveling together. Freda has the cabin next door to mine."

"I'm Jerome Sanchez, security officer, and this is Ray Parkinson, ship's doctor. Can you tell us how you came to find the body?"

"We didn't exactly find the body," Pauline said. "We were returning from dinner and I saw him lying in the shadows. I didn't really know it was a body at that stage."

"Is this how you found him?" Sanchez asked.

"Yes," Pauline responded. "Just as I found him."

"You didn't move the body?"

"I checked his pulse at wrist and throat," Pauline replied. "I discovered some small amount of blood in his beard and lifted his chin. He appears to have a narrow wound there. It's hard to be certain with the beard."

Pauline watched as the doctor continued examining the body, gently raising the man's chin to observe the wound. She was irritated by the fact the doctor wasn't wearing gloves. He was damaging the crime scene. Then she remembered she'd done the same and banished the thought from her mind.

"What will you do?" she asked the security officer, who looked bemused by events.

"I'll have to report to the captain. He will then check with the head office," Sanchez said. "There are procedures for this but I'm not sure they've ever been used. A death, possibly murder, on our first cruise! It's a disaster."

"We won't have to turn back, will we?" Freda asked.

"I don't think so," Sanchez said, "but we will do whatever the procedure says. I haven't read it yet. To be honest, I couldn't believe there was a death onboard. I hope it will prove to be an accident or some other understandable occurrence."

The doctor stood up, saying "We should move the body to our medical center."

"But the police will need to see the undisturbed crime scene," Pauline reminded him.

"The police can't come on board until tomorrow," Sanchez said, "and we can't leave the body here all that time."

"Then you need to get the ship's photographers to come and take photos," Pauline replied sharply.

"Good idea," Sanchez said, brightening now that he had some positive course of action to follow. "I'll get them here immediately."

"They have to understand they can't touch anything," Pauline said.

"Of course," he replied, "of course. This has thrown me completely. I can't think straight. We need to keep everyone away from here until a photographer has captured the scene and then we can move the body to the medical bay, Doctor."

"Someone must stay with the body."

"Will you do that, Doctor?" Sanchez asked. "And I'll get the photographer, plus instructions from the captain and company. As well, Doctor, you may want to consider if Miss Riddell and Mrs. Holman require any medical attention."

"We do not," Pauline snapped. "We are both quite familiar with dead bodies. Freda is a nurse and I'm a consulting detective."

"Then I will leave you and send a security officer to stand guard over the body so you, Doctor, can make the arrangements to move it," Sanchez said. He hurried away, much to Pauline's relief. She didn't think highly of either of the two men, though she thought Sanchez at least respectable.

An officer stepped out onto the deck and came toward them. She was a tall, blonde woman with a stern expression. Eastern European, Pauline thought, and she was right. Her name badge said, 'Nina, Poland.' One of those fleeing the Eastern Bloc as the iron grip of its rulers frayed.

"I have come to relieve you of your guard duties, Doctor," the woman said.

"Is a photographer coming?" Pauline asked. Though Sanchez had earlier hinted she should leave, she was determined to stay until she'd seen the body properly photographed. None of those assembled had any idea what crime scene photographs needed to capture.

"Yes. He just has to get the right equipment. He'll be here soon," Nina said. "You should return inside. It is growing cold."

"We shall do that as soon as I've advised the photographer what needs to be photographed and I've seen him do so," Pauline said. "I have some expertise in these matters, you see."

Nina shrugged and turned away to speak to the doctor who was preparing to leave. Before he did, Pauline saw the photographer step out from the lounge farther down the deck and into the darkness. He was carrying lights as well as his camera and for that Pauline was grateful. He, at least, had thought about his job and prepared accordingly.

Once the area was lit, the photo taking went quickly. The young photographer seemed happy to accept Pauline's advice as she directed him to the body's chin, hands, and unusual angle of the neck. She also suggested photos of the railings and decks of the two floors above from where the man must have fallen.

Sanchez and the captain returned, and Pauline advised the captain he should have the relevant areas on all three decks roped off. Police from the first stop at the Islands would want to see them before deciding if this warranted further investigation.

The captain wasn't put out by this at all. "I'd heard you were something of a celebrity in the criminal investigation world, Miss Riddell. I see that is true. You have experience in these matters."

"I couldn't have afforded to be on this trip if I wasn't a celebrity, to use your word, Captain," Pauline said. "And, yes, I do have practice. However, I understand there's a police detective among the passengers as well. Unless your company wishes to hire me, I suggest you approach him as a more official sounding representative. The local police may find my involvement unacceptable. Police often do, I'm afraid."

"I will take your advice, Miss Riddell, but I am going to put your name forward to our head office should we have need of an investigator. The incident happened in international waters, on a Bahamian-registered ship, operated by a Canadian travel company. I'm not sure who would be best to look into this if it turns out to be something other than an accident."

"I should warn you, and your head office; my fees are high nowadays and I don't accept anything but the truth. For me, the law must be adhered to. However imperfect it often is, it is our only hope of maintaining civilization in the long run."

"We can discuss all this if the need arises, Miss Riddell," the captain said. "Now, I can see you're both shivering with cold. Please go inside and get warm. We don't need you falling ill and adding to our difficulties."

As the photographer had taken all the photos Pauline wanted, she agreed this was a sensible thing to do, so she and Freda hurried away.

5
―――――――――――

NEXT MORNING. AT SEA

"THANK YOU FOR JOINING US, Miss Riddell," the captain said as Pauline entered the room. "You know detective Jason Somerville from the Toronto Police Force, I think?"

"We met at dinner last night," Pauline said coldly but accepted the detective's outstretched hand and shook it. The detective's expression suggested he was also not pleased, though his handshake was firm enough.

The captain continued, "As you know, if you've read the literature in your cabin or been listening to me over the ship's public address system, I'm Bill Ferguson, captain of this fine vessel, MS Orillia. Now, please take a seat both of you while I fill you in on what the company would like of you."

When his two guests were comfortable, he continued, "We will be in Puerto Ayora in another hour and I've already made the Ecuadorean police aware of what has occurred. With the information that is available from the witnesses and the ship's doctor, I've told the police it was an accident." He looked at Pauline to see if she was going to object.

Pauline, though she believed it wasn't a simple accident, wasn't prepared to challenge this decision.

"If the police accept this as an accident, though I'm sure they will also investigate," the captain said, "we anticipate that the cruise will be allowed to continue without serious interruption. Perhaps we will be a few more hours in Puerto Ayora than we would normally stay, but we can catch the time up overnight." He paused for comments. When there were none, he continued, "Miss Riddell, however, noticed a cut under the dead man's chin that might suggest it wasn't a simple accident." He paused again.

Pauline said, "You said *cut*, Captain. Am I to understand there was only a superficial injury there?"

"That's correct, Miss Riddell. Doctor Parkinson examined this wound carefully and assures me it is shallow and had no part in the victim's death."

"Not directly, perhaps," Pauline said, frowning. She'd been sure it was more serious.

"Which brings me to the point of this meeting," the captain said. "We are going to present everything we have to the authorities along with our belief it was an accident. The company, however, would like you both, individually or together, to investigate further during the rest of the cruise, if we're allowed to proceed."

"Why?" the detective asked. "It can only make people unhappy and create trouble. If you believe it's an accident say so and stick with that."

"We appreciate that, Detective, but the company feels it would be better for us to find any anomalies rather than being surprised if the police do. Are either of you, or better yet, both of you, interested in taking on this challenge?"

"I'm here on vacation, Captain, with my recently widowed sister," Pauline said. "If Detective Somerville is happy to take it on, that will be good enough for me. I do, however, applaud the company in wanting to get to the bottom of this. That cut under the victim's chin is unlikely to have been from a fall."

"Tell me more about this cut," Somerville said.

"Miss Riddell found a cut under the man's chin, which she feels in some way contributed to his death," Captain Ferguson said. "It was such a minor cut that hardly seems possible, but it has raised doubts in my mind, which is why I persuaded the company to have you both investigate properly. I hope, Miss Riddell, you will look into this, if only as a favor to me."

The detective looked puzzled. "I think Miss Riddell should do as she suggested and enjoy her cruise. You'll have better acceptance of your case, whatever I find, if it comes from a professional."

"Miss Riddell is a professional detective," the Captain said.

"Not a qualified one. Not even a qualified private investigator, as I understand it."

The captain looked at Pauline for confirmation.

"Detective Somerville is correct, Captain. As I don't work for the police or practice as a Private Investigator, I've never seen any need to study for the private investigator qualification nor the police qualifications." Pauline had already heard enough from Detective Somerville to know they couldn't work together. "All I do is what any other citizen can do at any time, which is think, analyze and provide my conclusions to the police."

"Nevertheless, Miss Riddell, you have a considerable reputation in these matters over many years, I implore you to look into this for me."

"We could each do our own investigation, Captain," Somerville said. "We can report to you regularly and when we're complete, I expect we'll have found the same result. That will be even further reassurance for your company, I think."

Captain Ferguson again looked to Pauline for her assent.

"As it is you asking, Captain, and not the company's Board of Directors, I will give the event some of my time but I repeat, I'm here to support my sister at a difficult time for her, not investigate a suspicious death."

"Then please, both of you, proceed in your own way," the captain said. "I shall invite you both to my office each evening after dinner to hear your progress."

Somerville practically leapt from his chair and took a hurried leave of them both. "I must see the body and speak to the doctor," he said, "before the police come aboard."

"A very precipitate young man," Pauline said.

"Isn't he just," Ferguson replied. "Nevertheless, his energy and passion will bring rewards, I'm sure."

"And you, Captain," Pauline asked, "did your energy and passion bring you rewards?"

"You mean what's a man of my age and experience doing shuttling tourists from the mainland to the Galapagos Islands, so far from home?"

"More or less," Pauline said. "We're from the same part of the world and one of my brothers is a captain too, so I'm interested."

"I know your brother Matt. We've sailed together as officers over the years, which is why I know of you, Miss Riddell. He's very proud of you," Ferguson added, grinning.

Pauline flushed pink. "Matt is one of my biggest fans," she said, "and, I fear, like all fans, he may overrate my abilities and achievements."

"And you may underrate them, as is proper, of course. We should none of us brag about ourselves. But to answer your question, I was captain of this ship when it was the MS Ilium and taking tourists around the Eastern Mediterranean. I've been with her since the Sixties when it was all happening on the Greek Islands. We took school trips in the spring and autumn season; they were fun too. It was a happy time."

"And now?"

"The Eighties haven't been kind to any of us, passengers or crew, and the ship was to be scrapped and me with it. With things as they are at home right now, unemployment in double digits and marine unemployment even more than that, the British merchant fleet gone, it looked like the end of my working life. Then a miracle happened."

"The tour company bought the ship?"

"They did and had it refitted for a more upmarket clientele. Where we used to have cabins for three hundred guests, now it's only ninety. Where we had entertainment for regular folk, now we have lectures for people who love nature and photography. I'm not ashamed to say I practically begged them to take me with the ship. After all, no one, other than our chief engineer, knows her better. They agreed so here I am. In nine more years, I can retire and draw my pension so I'm hoping very much this new venture succeeds."

"Which is why you're keen to have no shadow of wrongdoing to destroy the company's future?"

"Yes, I'm afraid my desire for a satisfactory answer here is personal as well as professional."

"I will do my best for you, Captain," Pauline said, "but I'll report what I find, even if that causes you and the company harm. I'm sorry I can't do otherwise. My conscience would never let me."

"Miss Riddell, I would never ask you to. I'm old-fashioned enough to believe that if someone has been murdered, justice must be done."

Pauline rose. "Then I wish you good day, Captain, until I return to report my progress."

She left the cabin and returned to the lounge where Freda was in deep discussion with an elderly widow. Pauline sighed. Misery may love company but too much of its company isn't good for anyone. She caught Freda's eye and drew her away.

"You should have joined us," Freda said, as they walked toward the bar where tea and coffee were being served. "Mrs. Schomberg is nice."

"I want to tell you of my meeting with the captain and I can't do that with people about," Pauline said.

"Oh. I'd forgotten about that."

They took their tea outside where the sunshine seemed to pin them to the planking. They climbed the steps leading to the first of the decks from where Jose could have fallen and made their way to the spot. Once they were in an area clear enough to see they weren't observed or likely to be overheard, Pauline told Freda she was investigating the suspicious death of Jose.

"Polly, are you sure you want to do this?"

"The Captain knows Matt and has asked for my help," Pauline said. "Anyway, if this young man was murdered, he deserves that we find out who did it and see that they are punished."

"But Polly, you're sticking your neck out here. Everyone says it's an accident. If you can't prove it isn't, your own standing, your reputation if you like, will be tarnished."

"So be it," Pauline said. "No one other than the people on this ship will know so my reputation, as you call it, won't suffer any damage."

"People always know. Remember, many of the passengers are from Toronto as well. Word will get about. You've become quite famous there since that jewel robbery crime you solved."

"Maybe it's time for me to hang up my deerstalker and magnifying glass anyhow. I don't know how Miss Marple kept it going into her seventies."

"Then quit right now and save my holiday."

Pauline shook her head. "I can't," she said. "That young man had the face of an angel. I must bring his killer to justice. I must."

"That's the end of our holiday together," Freda said, her expression gloomy.

"There will be plenty of time together," Pauline said. "After all, my investigating will be done here on the ship."

"That's true," Freda said, and added, brightening, "and I can help. I've always been a bit jealous of your detective work. We'll be a detecting team."

Pauline smiled. "We'll be a detective team," she agreed, "when we're not photographing iguanas and finches. We're starting right now by revisiting the possible crime scenes."

They found the railing above the place Jose had been lying and looked over.

"It's not high enough," Freda said. "If he fell awkwardly, he could die, of course, but it isn't more than fifteen feet. If it's murder, the murderer took an awful chance."

Pauline nodded. "You're already thinking like a detective," she said. "We're going to be a great team. As you say, to be certain, a murderer would want it to be from the next deck up. Maybe it wasn't really murder. Maybe someone pushed him, he overbalanced on the railing and plunged to his death and the someone was horrified at what they'd done."

"If it was an accident," Freda said, "wouldn't they have gone for help?"

"You or I would," Pauline said, "but many people are just frightened of what could happen to them, or they could have some reason to believe the authorities wouldn't believe it was an accident. I agree it's unlikely, but we can't rule it out. Let's go up to the next deck."

The upper deck was windy causing their hair and skirts to flap around them.

"I don't like it up here with this stiff breeze," Freda said. "I feel I'm going to be blown overboard."

Pauline didn't reply. She'd reached the point from where Jose might have fallen, and she was gently shaking the loose gate in the railing.

"This is where he fell from," Pauline said. Freda slowly joined her and held onto the rail rather than the gate. She looked over.

"I agree," she said. "A thirty-foot drop onto hard, wooden planking. He wouldn't have survived even if he'd gone face first rather than backwards, as the position of the body and the injuries suggested."

Pauline nodded. "I think he was forced against this gate by someone holding a knife under his chin. Then, either the gate moved behind him and he overbalanced or the someone pushed him and over he went."

They continued staring down at the deck below, remembering the body as it lay there the night before.

"There's nowhere for him to have got that cut under his chin," Freda said. "There are cables and metal beams but nothing with a sharp edge."

"No," Pauline said. "It was definitely a knife or something very like it."

"It still could be an accident, or manslaughter anyway," Freda said, unwilling to accept she was sharing a ship with a killer.

"It can't be an accident, but it could be manslaughter rather than murder," Pauline agreed. "Our job is to find out which and why."

For a moment, they examined the deck around the gate, and nearby corners and crevices. There was nothing. The ship was too newly recommissioned for much of any kind of litter to be hiding out.

"What do we do now?" Freda asked.

"We ask questions," Pauline replied. "The captain said Jose Garcia, that was his family name by the way, was a member of the maintenance crew, so we start there."

"But we've never seen any of the maintenance crew," Freda objected.

"You haven't been looking," Pauline said. "Remember the man working in the cabin along our corridor? Or the men changing the layout of the lounge after dinner last night and breakfast this morning?"

"Oh, yes. I see. I was thinking of the people running the engines and things."

"I think they're engineering," Pauline said. "We'll walk the decks until we find a willing volunteer. There'll be crew about after we dock." The ship was approaching a harbor mouth and a pilot vessel was approaching.

"Won't the police be interviewing them then?"

"Maybe," Pauline agreed, "and if they are, we'll wait until later. We need to know who Jose was and who his friends and colleagues were."

"You said the captain told you this was a maiden voyage for the ship and tour company," Freda said. "He may not have had either."

"Someone knew him well enough to stick a knife under his chin and cause him to fall over a railing," Pauline said. "That isn't the action of someone you've just met. That requires a history of love or hate."

They watched as the ship was guided to its berth and tied up. When it was secure, a gangplank was placed, and police came aboard.

"More tea, I think," Pauline said, "and one of those nice pastries I saw them putting out as we came through the lounge." At breakfast, the guests had been told they couldn't disembark until the authorities had given permission for them to leave.

"They'll be all gone by now," Freda said. "We should have had one before we came up here."

"North Americans eat cakes," Pauline said. "There are always pastries left." She was right. Fortunately, they'd finished their tea and macaroon when the call came for them to go to the captain's cabin, a call they'd been expecting because they had found the body.

With the aid of an interpreter, they described the scene as they'd found it. The police captain asked, "You heard no cry or the noise of the body hitting the deck?"

"No, we heard nothing. We were on the deck for a few minutes before I saw him," Pauline said.

"You said the time was about twenty hundred hours," the police captain said, "and you saw no one else about."

"That's correct," Pauline said. "We finished dinner, sat over coffee before taking a stroll. It was a cool night, quite surprisingly cold really, and I imagine anyone who'd come out had hurried back inside."

"The moon was bright, you said."

"It was but shining on the other side of the ship. The side nearest our cabins, where we finished our walk, was shadowy. Not dark but the man was lying in a place where the lifeboats provided shadow from the moon and starlight and the deck lights."

"The doctor says you thought he'd been stabbed."

"I did. When I saw blood on my fingers after checking for a pulse at his throat, I assumed he'd been stabbed with an upward thrust from a knife," Pauline said. "Then, after Freda, who is a nurse, checked, she realized his neck was broken."

"And did that change your mind about murder?"

"No," Pauline said. "I just thought he'd been stabbed and then fallen. The fall broke his neck after he was dead." Seeing where the police captain was going, she decided to speed things up. "It wasn't until I heard that the wound under his chin was just a cut, that I realized he hadn't died that way."

"So, you no longer think he was murdered?"

"I don't know how he died, Captain," Pauline said. "I only know it wasn't the way I thought when I first found him."

The police captain nodded. "Thank you, Señorita. Your assistance has been invaluable."

Pauline and Freda left the cabin in silence. Once away from there, however, Freda said, "You didn't tell him you still think Jose was killed and didn't die in an accident."

"He didn't persist in his question about my murder theory and I have no proof to give it credence. It's best we let the local authorities manage things in their own way," Pauline said. "If only in the hope it means we can have our holiday together without further delay."

"Pauline!" Freda said, shocked. "After all you said, you can't mean that."

Pauline frowned. "Don't misunderstand me, Freddy, I take all violent deaths very seriously, but the most likely explanation is this man, Jose, was part of some sordid criminal enterprise and he paid for it with his life. It is for local people to manage their own affairs. We will investigate but not become embroiled in the local investigation or point them in directions we're only guessing at."

"But surely we should help where we can?" Freda protested.

"Help, by all means, but their law is their law. They understand the underpinnings where we don't," Pauline said. "I believe in the law; it's all any society has to keep itself stable. But laws are specific to time and place and should not be tampered with by those who don't understand either."

"I suspect our laws are kinder and more compassionate," Freda said, still brooding on yesterday's incident at the marketplace. "Wouldn't we make things better by helping them see that? If their laws matched ours, you would be outraged by what we witnessed the other day instead of just accepting it."

"As I said, all customs and laws work in their own context," Pauline said. "It doesn't follow they would be successful in a different time or place. If we implemented our customs and laws here, as we tried to do in so many other places up until recently, we would create the backlash we've already seen all around the world and will see more of in future. The number of people dead may be just as high thanks to our meddling as if we'd left well enough alone. We are visitors here, not conquerors and we have no business interfering."

"But, Pauline…"

"No buts," Pauline said. "We can't just step off a plane in someone else's country and start dictating to them."

Freda sighed. They were never going to agree on this. Pauline was always so aloof and distant. She never could see that sometimes you had to guide people for their own good.

6

SANTA CRUZ AND GIANT TORTOISES

AS THE BREAKFAST was being served, Captain Ferguson's voice boomed over the ship's public address system.

"Good morning, everyone. I hope you had a good night's sleep on your first night at sea and you're awake and refreshed for the day ahead, which will be a little different from that outlined in our itinerary. Please listen carefully while I explain.

"As most of you will know by now, we had an unfortunate accident onboard last night. One of the crew fell to his death and we've put into Puerto Ayora, the capital of the Galapagos Islands, to report the incident and transfer the body ashore. The Ecuadorean police will come aboard soon and they will be here for some time investigating the incident. I hope we won't be held up too long.

"However, they may want us to stay in port at least for today. Rather than waste a day of your vacation, we have brought forward the final day's activities. As you know, the giant tortoises are the heart of the Galapagos, indeed they're what give the islands their name, and they were intended to be the crowning event on the last day of the cruise. Instead, to ensure you don't miss these magnificent creatures, we will visit the Charles Darwin Station today and see and learn more about these gentle giants.

"The tour will spend half the day there and then you will be free to spend the rest of the day in town where you can enjoy sightseeing, souvenir shopping and meeting the local people. We do apologize for this change, but it is beyond our control. I'm confident our delay will be short and we'll sail tonight. Those of you who have purchased your excursion tickets for the tortoise breeding station, please make your way to deck three before eight-thirty am. Those of you who haven't and wish to do so…"

"Well," said Pauline, as the announcement went into details they had no need of, "they were the highlight of the trip for me. Everything else will seem an anti-climax now."

"Surely not," Freda said, aghast at such heresy. "It's the finches and the iguanas that are key to the Galapagos story."

Pauline smiled. "I know that's true, and I know I should value them as you do but we have finches at home, and iguanas, however cleverly adapted, are still just lizards and not my cup of tea."

Freda shook her head in dismay at this levity. "Then we should get our tickets and be on deck number three because you can't afford to miss the only bit you're interested in. This announcement has already left it very late."

"I suspect the Captain has only just been told by the police that the ship can't drop off a body and sail on as if nothing happened," Pauline said. "Hence this scramble to make use of the day."

"You didn't find some way to tell the police it was murder, did you?" Freda said, laughing.

"I did tell them that was what I thought at first but I don't believe police anywhere just accept 'accident' as an explanation when notified about a death. I think we'll be lucky to sail tonight."

* * *

"ARE YOU GLAD NOW WE CAME?" Freda said, as she took a photo of Pauline beside the largest tortoise on the hillside. The tortoise continued munching the coarse grass as if unaware people were lining up to have it star in their vacation pictures.

"I am. I'll even properly appreciate the iguanas now," Pauline agreed, as she exchanged places with Freda.

"They are huge, aren't they?" Freda said, timidly touching the shell that reached as high as her waist.

"And unbelievably placid," Pauline said. "No wonder sailors on the Pacific stopped in at the Galapagos all those centuries ago. The fresh meat here just waits to be eaten."

"Oh don't," Freda said with a shudder. "How could anyone treat such harmless creatures that way?"

"You haven't been hungry enough, Freddie, or you'd know the answer to that question."

They gave up their spot to the next people waiting in line and meandered through the park. Other, not so ancient or so large, tortoises cropped the grass between the trees, testament to the success of the breeding program. In places, they could see what looked like fields of trees outside the breeding station.

"What do you think they are?" Freda said.

"If you'd been listening to the guide," Pauline said, "you'd know there are coffee plantations farther up the hillside. I think that's what they are."

"Hmm, probably. If the police are happy it was an accident, Polly, will you continue investigating?"

"I plan to because it might set Captain Ferguson's mind at ease. But really, it's nothing to do with us and, as I said, I'm sure there's a very sordid answer to this death that has nothing to do with the ship's company or the cruise line."

"But the murderer may stay on the ship," Freda said.

"Unlikely. Their job is done. They will leave when the voyage is over and return to their gang."

"In my work, I've patched up all sorts of victims of accidents and diseases but rarely human violence," Freda said, thinking aloud.

"That's because you worked in rural Cottage Hospitals," Pauline said. "If you'd been in a city hospital, you would."

"You would think we could all get along, wouldn't you, with all this beauty around us."

"You're growing sentimental, Freddie. It isn't described as 'nature, red in tooth and claw' because the world is a beautiful place."

After the tortoise breeding center, wandering the small town was disappointing. Tourism was only getting a foothold, but the main street already had more gift shops than regular stores. They spent some time viewing ponchos and lace headdresses before continuing back to the quay.

Like quaysides at home, there was a busy fish market but here there was lots more to see and not just in the greater selection of seafood than they were used to.

"Those pelicans begging for scraps are funny," Pauline said, as they watched the huge birds hopping from floor to countertop like sparrows at a picnic.

"Not very hygienic," Freda replied, grimacing, her hospital training to the fore.

Pauline laughed. "Then don't eat the ceviche at dinner tonight."

"Oh, Lord. I had that last night, didn't I?"

"You did but I'm sure the fish didn't come from this market."

"It could have come from one very like it, though, couldn't it?"

"The tour company will have been very careful to keep our Western tummies safe, you can be sure," Pauline said.

"I hope you're right, but I won't be eating raw fish again."

"Let's walk to the end of the pier and get away from these distressing sights," Pauline said, laughing at her sister's pained expression.

As they approached the end of the pier, however, they saw Arvin Weiss staring into the shelter intended to protect people from the wind.

"Most people would look out over the harbor," Freda said, shaking her head in disbelief, "but not Arvin. Should we turn around?"

"It's too late," Pauline replied. "He's seen us and wants us to join him."

Arvin was waving them to come but in a strange slow-motion way that suggested great care.

"What do you think is in that shelter?" Freda asked.

Pauline laughed. "Can it be worse than pelicans on fish market counters?"

"Hello, Arvin," Freda began as they neared him.

He put his finger to his lips.

Pauline and Freda could now see inside the shelter. Lying full-length along a bench made for at least six people was a seal, its brown fur drying in the sun, and a dignified but unamused expression on its face.

Freda quickly took a photo. "I don't think it likes being disturbed," she said.

"It *is* rude of us to stare," Pauline agreed.

"How did it get there?" Arvin said. "That's what beats me."

"It's obviously more agile on land than we think seals should be," Pauline said, "but I agree, how did it do that?"

"Practice," Freda said. "It probably suns itself here every fine day."

"Nobody would fight it for the seat, that's for sure," Arvin said, grinning.

It was the first time Pauline had seen Arvin enjoying himself and it made her feel ridiculously pleased for him.

Freda walked around the back of the shelter. "There isn't one this side," she called, "but there's no sun either." She returned to join the other two who were still watching the seal who glared back impassively, daring them to shoo it away.

The seal yawned, displaying a fine set of sharp pointed flesh-tearing teeth and the three stepped back as one.

"I think we should leave it to its rest," Pauline said, turning away.

Arvin too set off with them. "Do you really think it lies there every day?"

"Whenever it wants to, I imagine," Pauline said. "I don't think people here eat seals so it's quite safe."

"You would think the locals would want to sit in the sun some days, weekends, maybe," Arvin said.

"Would you want to sit there now? You'd never get the smell out of your clothes."

"I guess not," Arvin agreed. "Still, having a shelter you can't use must be a real bummer for the locals."

"Maybe people here like seals more than sunshine," Freda said.

"Could be," Arvin said. "Say, did you ladies hear anything more about the death on board last night?"

"No," Pauline said quickly. "Why, did you?"

"The police were grilling the crew pretty hard when I came ashore. I thought there may be more to it than an accident."

"You didn't see the tortoises then?"

"Nah, ugly brutes. I knew somebody who had one when I

was a kid. It was a little one, not a big one. It did nothing but eat, sleep and poop so far as I could tell. Can't imagine a giant one would be any different."

Pauline smiled. "Not a lot different, that's true. I'm not sure they even knew we were there, to be honest. People were milling around them, but they just went on eating."

"Then I saved myself the cost of the excursion," Arvin said. "You relieved my mind."

"To the matter you mentioned earlier, the death on board," Pauline said, "did you see or hear anything odd last night?"

"Me? Why would I?"

"No reason, I just wondered. You'd think some of us would have heard or seen something."

"Most of our fellow passengers are so old they wouldn't hear if a bomb fell, let alone a body."

"You're probably right," Pauline agreed, "and the lounge was loud with music and conversation. People were finally relaxing after the journey to get here."

"It was too loud for me and I didn't feel too good," Arvin said. "I had an early night."

"And today you're refreshed and raring to explore," Freda said.

"Well, happy enough to get off the boat and wander the streets. I get nervous when I see police uniforms."

"Where did you learn to distrust the police?" Pauline asked.

"Growing up in Germany, during and after the war," Arvin said. "My family were lucky and were given permission to go to Israel."

"That would have been better, I'm sure," Pauline said.

Arvin's expression remained grim. "Not really," he said. "The police were on our side, that's true, but lots of others weren't, so it was just as frightening. I left the moment I got the chance. You see, I've been running all my life."

"We're back at the landing place," Freda said, diplomatically changing the subject. "Are we going back on board or do you want to walk some more, Polly?"

"I think I'll go back," Pauline said. "It's hot now. A cold drink and some shade would be very welcome."

* * *

IN THE EVENING, the passengers were gathered into the lounge to hear from the captain in person.

"Good evening, ladies and gentlemen," Captain Ferguson began, "I hope you all enjoyed your day on Santa Cruz and, in particular, the Charles Darwin Center." He paused while his audience enthusiastically assured him they had.

"The unhappy event of last night, which the police are now happy was indeed an accident, has thrown our intended itinerary and required us to re-plan your cruise." An unhappy silence greeted this statement and Ferguson pressed on quickly. "Have no fear, you will see all the places you chose to see when you signed up for the trip, we will just be doing them in reverse order. Other groups have been moved forward to take the spots we weren't able to take because of this forced day in port."

"The good news is, we have been cleared to sail in another hour. Our first landfall tomorrow morning will be on the small island of South Plaza. You've all come to see marine iguanas but, on this island, you'll see the opposite: iguanas as they exist everywhere else on this planet, that is, on land. Those of you who have bought tickets for this tour, please be ready to disembark by eight-thirty a.m."

Instantly a babble of questions arose as people wanted to get clarification. Many had not heard what he said accurately, many hadn't been listening at all. Pauline's heart sank. The thought of nine more days of people not hearing, while others refused to even listen, was setting her teeth on edge. Finally, there was calm and Ferguson was able to continue.

"We will be issuing a new itinerary as soon as they are printed," he said, "but keep the old ones for the information they contain. The new itinerary will only include the names, dates and times of the stops because we have no professional printers on board to redo the whole pamphlet." Once again, the passengers fell to talking among themselves and the noise level was too high for him to speak and be heard.

When it quieted, he continued, "The area where the crewman fell from has been roped off while the Engineering & Maintenance crews make and install a new gate. This will only be for today or part of tomorrow at the latest. Meanwhile, I would ask you to keep well away from the area. If the ship were to roll suddenly, you may also fall against the gate and possibly fall to the deck below."

"If the gate is dangerous," a passenger called out, "why wasn't it fixed before we sailed? And how can we be sure other gates aren't also unsafe?"

"A full investigation is being made into the circumstances around the gate and how it came to be as it was," Captain Ferguson replied, "and I've had officers and local safety inspectors examine every similar gate and railing on the ship throughout the day. I'm assured there is no other hazard."

"Even if the gate is made safe, Captain, how can we be sure there isn't a murderer onboard? The police were very quick to call this an accident," another passenger asked.

"They were quick to call it an accident because all the evidence suggests it was. There's nothing to say he wasn't alone when he fell or that anyone onboard wished him harm," Captain Ferguson replied. "But your question is one I and the company would also like answered. Can we be absolutely sure that Jose Garcia was not pushed?" There was further murmuring, which he let die down before he continued.

"As some of you may know, we have onboard no less than two detectives, both highly regarded in their own way. The company has asked them to investigate the occurrence and provide some additional assurance that the police were correct in their assessment. I hope you will help them in any way you can."

Captain Ferguson asked Detective Somerville and Pauline to stand, introduced them with some details of their careers, before urging the passengers to remember their faces and answer any questions they might have.

"What if you find there is a murderer onboard?" a passenger asked Somerville.

"Then we'll notify the captain, and he will notify the authorities," Somerville replied. "Remember, Miss Riddell and I are also passengers on the ship. If we find a murderer, as detectives, we're even more at risk than you are."

"Does this ship have a jail?" was the follow-up question.

Captain Ferguson replied, "We have a secure cabin that we keep for those highly unusual cases where isolation of a passenger or crew member is needed. We've never used it in all my time on the ship and I don't believe we will this time either."

The subdued conversations that followed this suggested the passengers weren't as happy with the idea of an investigation as Captain Ferguson had hoped they would be.

He continued, "I'm not going to sugar-coat this," he said, "this isn't a nice thing to have hanging over us on what should have been a joyful vacation, but I ask you once again to take part in this honestly. If there is a threat to others on board, it's best we know sooner rather than later. You may have heard of 'Mystery Nights' or 'Mystery Cruises' where the guests take part in a murder mystery performance. Try to think of it in that light, and I hope that's how it will be seen at the end of the investigation but please keep in mind, in this case, it isn't just a parlor game. Please help Detectives Somerville and Riddell as much as you can."

As he finished speaking, the Cruise Director arrived with a folder of revised itineraries and the conversation immediately switched to that and the changes. Captain Ferguson left quietly, leaving the Director to explain the new route.

As they left the lounge, making their way out onto the deck to enjoy the night air and stars, Pauline heard herself being called. She looked about and saw Detective Somerville on a higher deck signaling her to join him.

"You stay here with the others and enjoy the drinks and snacks, Freddie. I'll go and see what he wants and see you back at the cabins."

She climbed the steps up to the deck where Somerville was waiting. She'd vowed to herself she would always use the stairs and not the elevators or she'd be pounds heavier by the time the cruise was over. Sometimes, she wished she wasn't quite so diligent in carrying out her vows.

"What is it," Pauline said, puffing a little and embarrassed because of it, "that couldn't wait until tomorrow?"

"I wanted to ask you about finding the body," Somerville said to Pauline, ushering her into the Purser's office and to a chair.

"Really," Pauline said bluntly. Her opinion of the man was low from the moment they'd met at dinner the night before and it sank even lower by his commanding her to this meeting; it had been uncourteously done. She thought his appearance also didn't inspire confidence. He was poorly groomed, badly and inappropriately dressed in a Hawaiian shirt of gaudy flowers and parrots, and seemingly unable to understand how unprofessional all that looked.

"I wanted to ask you to tell me everything that happened before, during and after you discovered the body, up until the time the security officer and doctor arrived," Somerville said. "We didn't really talk when the captain brought us together."

"I've already provided a written a statement on this to the captain and the police," Pauline replied, "have you not seen it?"

"The captain shared it with me, but I'd rather hear it from you and explore your memory for more details if you don't mind."

"Very well," Pauline said. She hadn't believed it possible but she was beginning to like him even less. Did he really think she hadn't already done this?

She began recounting the events of the previous evening, from the moment she and Freda decided they would return to their cabins. Somerville listened quietly until she reached the point where she'd discovered the body.

"Did you call for help immediately after you found the body?"

"Not immediately," Pauline said coldly, "as I said in my statement. I wasn't sure of the man's condition. I checked his pulse at his wrist and then at his neck. That's when I found blood on my fingers and I discovered he'd been stabbed under his chin."

"And you heard and saw no one?"

"That's correct," Pauline replied, "From the moment I saw it was a body and not a pile of clothes, I was very alert for sounds and the sight of anyone else. I'm not without experience in these matters."

"I'm sure you've thought about this, so I won't beat about the bush," Somerville said, "From a detection point of view those who last saw the victim or are first on the scene are likely to be involved in some way with the crime. To be clear, I'm not accusing you of anything, but you must see that one explanation is that you did it."

Pauline frowned. She had expected this line of enquiry,

which is why she'd taken such trouble over her written statement.

"Well then, let me assure you I didn't," she said.

"Of course not," Somerville said, "but your explanation of how the victim got there would work if you'd caused him to fall and then come down to confirm he was dead."

"That's true," Pauline said, "though I should point out how slowly Freda and I would have come down two decks of steps. It would have been a crazy thing to do. Anyone could have heard him fall, come out to see what happened and would see us coming down the stairs."

"I think you would feel safe enough doing that, wouldn't you, Miss Riddell? Who would imagine two elderly ladies being capable of throwing a young man over a rail? I think you would just say you heard a noise and saw the body and were coming down to provide help. After all, Mrs. Holman is a trained nurse. And I understand how you might feel you're innocent, after all, as I see it, it wouldn't be murder, just self-defense."

Pauline was taken aback. This was very direct. "I can only repeat," she replied. "This man's death has nothing to do with me. I am interested in hearing your theory though."

"Okay, here's how I see it happening," Somerville said. "You were out for your after-dinner stroll, as you said, when the victim, who was passing and was perhaps overcome by his feelings, grabbed one of you, perhaps not realizing there were two of you. You, or Mrs. Holman, took something from your purse, scissors or a nail file maybe, and you stabbed him. You didn't mean to kill him, just fend him off, but he stepped back at that low place on the rail. He lost his balance and fell. Looking over the rail, you realized you may not have killed him and you hurried down to give him aid, perhaps. When you discovered he was dead and nobody had seen or heard anything, you decided to say you found him. Then once the security and doctor arrived you told them your story and explained the blood on your hands by saying you'd checked his pulse at his neck. You'd either pocketed the weapon and dropped it overboard later when the deck was clear or you threw it overboard as you came down the stairs. Is that close enough to how it happened? Nobody will blame you. It was just self-defense."

"That's a fine theory but I repeat, I had nothing to do with this man's death. Events happened as I described in my statement."

"But you can see where I'm coming from, can't you?"

"Yes, but there are too many holes in the story, Detective," Pauline said. "First, even allowing for the man's overwhelming youthful passion, which blinded him to the fact there were two of us and not one or that he could never get off the ship after what he'd done, do you really think he'd be driven to lust by the sight of one stringy, fifty-five-year-old woman or one plump woman who is even older, neither of whom were ever anything but plain?"

"Many people have unusual passions," Somerville replied, "Why not this one?"

"Very well," Pauline continued, "how did I, or Freda, have this weapon just there in our purses when it was needed. You suggest it was scissors or a nail file. You can check our dressing tables and find both are still very much in evidence."

"I only used scissors or a nail file as possible examples," the detective said, "until we have a proper post-mortem, we won't know what the weapon actually was."

"But somehow, you imagine, we were able to conceal this weapon throughout the time when the security officer and doctor were there and while my sister Freda was with me or that Freda wouldn't have seen me throw it overboard."

"I'm suggesting you are both supporting each other in this matter," Somerville said.

"Perhaps," Pauline said, "but all these small inconsistencies add up to an unlikely hypothesis, Detective."

"As I said, Miss Riddell, I'm not accusing you of anything, just testing theories."

"I'm pleased to hear it. Do you have any other theories that I can help you test?"

"None that you can help me with," the detective said, rather pompously for one so young.

Pauline stared at him in disbelief. The nerve of the man. He was barely out of school, hadn't a lick of sense, or an idea in his head, of that she was sure, and yet he took such airs to be above a mere amateur like her, even knowing how long she'd been working in this field.

"Then I'll leave you to continue investigating," Pauline said. "Should you wish to confirm we have all our sharp personal grooming tools, do ask. We'll both be happy to oblige."

Outside the office, Pauline found Freda, instead of socializing in the lounge, was waiting anxiously. "Is it all right?" she asked.

"Yes, of course," Pauline said. "He just wanted to talk about what we saw when we found the body, detective-to-detective so to speak."

"Oh," Freda said. "Will he want to speak to me, do you think?"

"Maybe," Pauline said, "but you should decline his invitation."

"Won't that upset him and make him suspicious?"

"Probably but I'm sure that young man is used to witnesses getting upset with him. Shall we go for tea and biscuits, though they'll call them cookies, while we learn more details of our next stop from the naturalist?"

"Don't you have a briefing with the captain?" Freda asked.

"Not until later, after the naturalist's talk. By then, I should be calm enough to meet Detective Somerville again without murdering him."

"Oh dear," Freda said. "You don't think it would be better to miss it tonight?"

"No dear, I don't. We will need to be on our toes with that young man. I can't leave him to manage the investigation alone. We will have to be involved."

"WELL, DETECTIVES," Captain Ferguson said, welcoming Pauline and Somerville to the briefing later that evening. "Have you learned anything that sheds light on this unfortunate affair?"

"Not a lot," Somerville said. "I interviewed the doctor and spent time with the Ecuadorean Police filling them in on details I'd seen at the two places of interest."

As he hadn't been present when the body was in one of those places of interest and the other was an empty deck, gate and railing, Pauline wondered how much updating he'd been able to provide the Ecuadorean Police. She didn't, however, share her musings.

"And you, Miss Riddell?"

"I've very little to add to what I've already said, Captain, but I would like you to provide us with some background on the dead man."

"I can give you what I've been told," Captain Ferguson said, "but I'll have to introduce you to the officer in charge of maintenance for more details. He was closer to the dead man, and the others of the maintenance crew, than I am."

"You give us the thirty-thousand-foot level, Captain," Somerville said, "and we'll get the finer details tomorrow."

"Very well. As I understand it, this is a tragic case. The young man was a refugee from Peru. You may have heard of the civil war between the government there and the Shining Path guerillas. It seems, when he was just a child, Jose's family was killed by government troops in an attack on their village, which the soldiers believed had been supporting the guerillas. After this horror, Jose was adopted by an uncle and aunt in another village and, some years later, when Jose was a teenager, that village was attacked by the Shining Path. His uncle and aunt and practically everyone in the village was killed. Jose was fortunate enough to be on his way to school when the attack began and was able to run and hide."

"Jeez," said Somerville, "how much bad luck can one guy have?"

"Quite!" Captain Ferguson said.

"He was carefully screened before he was hired, I presume," Pauline asked.

"Very carefully, I'm sure. The company can't afford to be lax when we have paying guests."

"Still," Somerville said, "one of the guys in your crew might be a wrong 'un and the dead man, Jose, may have recognized him. We need the background of all your crew, Captain, if we're going to be sure this wasn't murder."

"I'll have to get clearance from the head office for that. It will take a day or so."

"But we can talk to your officers about Jose, right?"

"I think that's a given. He's dead and you've been asked to investigate on our behalf."

"Good. Then I'll start first thing in the morning," Somerville said.

"Tomorrow is our first island stop," Captain Ferguson said. "Don't you want to be on the tour?"

"Oh! Right. Then the moment we get back."

"I'll have the maintenance and engineering officers available from two o'clock here in my cabin. Will you be taking part, Miss Riddell?"

"Certainly," Pauline said. "Now we know more about the victim, we have so many new possible motives to consider."

"Do you still think murder?"

"I think that's a possibility but not the only one."

The captain smiled. "I hope you won't mind me saying that I find your saying there may be other explanations is good news, Miss Riddell."

"I understand, Captain, but murder is still very much on my mind and if he was killed by a Shining Path extremist and that person is onboard this ship, we may be facing a more serious threat than any of us could imagine."

"What is this Shining Path?" Somerville asked.

"They're a particularly brutal guerilla organization, worse than almost any of the others anywhere in the world. They're Communists but also violent fanatics. Hearing that Jose was fleeing from them only makes me more certain his death wasn't an accident."

"Remember though, Jose was escaping from these people," Ferguson said, "and he was just a kid. Realistically, they aren't going to send a hitman after him. If he was important, the Peruvian government would have him in a safe place surrounded by guards."

"I hope you're right, Captain," Somerville said, "but what Miss Riddell just said scares me a bit. If there's any chance…"

"There isn't," Ferguson said. "It's madness to even think it."

"Unfortunately, Captain," Pauline said, "when searching for motives, we sometimes must think of the wildest things. I agree, a terrorist sent to kill Jose is extremely unlikely but until we have the solution to this mystery, I'll be wedging my cabin door shut with the furniture."

"I agree with you Captain," Somerville said. "Even though Jose was fleeing from them, communist guerillas are too unlikely. But back in Toronto, and most big cities, I guess, I see a lot of young kids who have run away from home and they get caught up in criminal gangs. Even though he wasn't running away from home in a traditional sense, Jose fits that pattern to a 'T'. I'd say we're more likely looking at drug gangs, or something like that, if there really is a hitman onboard."

"All of these possibilities make me even more determined to get to the bottom of what happened," Ferguson said. "Both of you need to get your investigations finished as quickly as you can, so we can all sleep easy in our beds."

"WHAT DID YOU TALK ABOUT TONIGHT?" Freda asked, when Pauline rejoined her in the lounge.

Her voice had a resentful edge. Pauline understood she felt excluded but had no intention of having her sister be part of the evening debriefing where Somerville could use Freda against her. "We'll talk outside," Pauline said. "Tonight's discussions were darker than is safe to share with the others."

They made their excuses and headed out onto the deck where there were fewer people. The evenings were perfect times to be out and about, in Pauline's mind, even though the sun sank quickly away. A purplish light in the sky outlined the islands briefly before darkness fell. Many sea creatures, dolphins chasing fish or maybe even whales, rose humpbacked to the surface of the luminescent water before sliding away into the depths. Most passengers missed it all, intent on the happy camaraderie that a shared experience and free-flowing drinks brought to people. Sometimes, she rather envied them that, but it soon passed.

"Well?" Freda demanded.

"More has come to light about Jose's background," Pauline said, and she recounted what they'd heard.

"Poor kid. I can't imagine what that would have been like."

"Quite so," Pauline said. "Poor kid indeed. Now I don't want to alarm you, Freddie, but I'm going to wedge my cabin door shut from now on. You should do the same."

"Why?"

"Because those monsters may have sent someone to kill him. They may feel they have to punish people who try to escape their group and that killer, hitman as Somerville says, may not like us investigating Jose's murder."

"Oh!" Freda said. "I thought this would be fun."

"Murder is never fun, Freddie. Grow up."

"But it wasn't murder, was it. It was just an accident. Only you thought it was murder."

"I thought it was murder," Pauline said stonily, "because it is murder." She shook her head in frustration.

"I suppose," Freda said, "I didn't really believe you. The police and everyone were so sure and you, well, had doubts."

"Always distrust people who are sure of things, Freddie. They haven't looked at all the evidence."

"It's all very well moralizing, Polly, but what now? You've been announced to the whole ship as an investigator and I'm right there alongside you."

"You're right, it is too late to escape now. We have to see it through to the end. And I may as well tell you the full extent of your potential danger. There's another possibility that I suggested to you at the outset and Detective Somerville outlined tonight. When he escaped from the terrorists, he may have become embroiled in criminal gangs in Lima or even Quito. Young people on the run often do. It could be that those people thought Jose had some knowledge, which could get them caught and it could be they, rather than guerillas, that have sent someone to silence him."

"Can this get any worse?" Freda cried.

"None of this is certain, Freddie. They're just possible avenues to be explored. We, however, need to be a bit more careful than usual for the next few days, that's all."

"That's all!"

"Yes! Don't go all hysterical on me or I'll regret having you on my detecting team."

"You can't regret it any more than I'm regretting being on your team right now." Freda cast an anxious glance around the empty deck. "Should we even be walking here alone?"

"There are two of us," Pauline said, "and this deck is well-lit and overlooked by the men on the bridge. We're as safe here as anywhere."

"That's probably what Jose thought when he wandered out onto an empty deck after sunset," Freda snapped.

"Stop it, Freddie. There's no sense talking this way."

"But it's why you said you didn't want to investigate in the first place. You said it was likely a sordid affair of Jose being involved with some criminals and they'd caught up with him. Now, because Detective Somerville says it, you're saying it's unlikely and I shouldn't worry."

"I said from now on you should wedge your cabin door shut and I'm not saying it's unlikely because Somerville said it. I'm just saying we need to keep a sense of proportion. If there's a gangland hitman, he won't want to bring attention to himself by killing someone else, particularly when the police have ruled it an accident."

"Urgh," Freda growled, and stalked off toward the cabins leaving Pauline in sole command of the deck.

"What did I say about being extra careful," she said, shaking her head. It was clearly a mistake involving Freda.

7

SOUTH PLAZA ISLAND

PAULINE AND FREDA woke early and made their way to Rise and Shine stretch class. Pauline had an added incentive for joining this class today, beyond just getting all the exercise they could to fight the layer of flab they'd accumulate if they didn't, judging by the meals and snacks that were continually being offered. Today, she wanted one last inspection of the railings and gate without anyone watching. Few people rose early on cruises, she'd noticed in the past, and just after sunrise would be especially quiet.

They were the only two in the class and, as Pauline had a pressing reason to finish it as quickly as possible, the moment it was over she thanked the instructor and marched Freda away.

"Quickly now," Pauline said, as they headed across the deck to where Jose fell.

"Why are we doing this?" Freda asked, eying the roped off gate with dislike.

"I want to look again at that gate and the railing during daylight and before the maintenance crew replaces it with a more substantial fix."

They stood for a moment in silence, inspecting the gate,

which was behind ropes and a warning sign. Pauline lifted the rope and, stooping, passed under it to stand at the railing. She looked down to the spot where Jose's body had lain the two nights before.

She turned to her sister, "Freddie, how tall are you?"

"Five feet, seven inches. Why?"

"You're that inch taller than me," Pauline said. "I'd like to test what that means with respect to the height of this gate."

"I'm not leaning on it to see if I fall over," Freda replied.

"I'm not asking you to," Pauline said. "Just stand beside it so I can see where it comes on your hip. The doctor said Jose was five feet, nine and a half inches. I can measure down you, to see where it would come on him."

Freda joined her sister at the railing and reluctantly allowed herself, holding tightly onto the railing at either side, to be positioned next to the gate while Pauline counted two-and-a-half inches down the back of her thigh.

"You see how low this would catch Jose and, being a man, with much more weight in the chest and shoulders and not so much in the hips—"

"Thank you very much!"

"I'm not making a comment about your hips, Freddie," Pauline said. "I'm just pointing out the top rail of this gate would be well below Jose's center-of-gravity. Once he toppled, he'd have little chance to save himself if he went over backwards, as I think he did."

"What does all this mean?"

"It means it wasn't an accident. Someone knew this gate was low and arranged this event to happen."

"It could still be an accident."

Pauline shook her head. "It's too fortuitous. We know there's nowhere else on the ship where this arrangement exists."

"Why does it exist at all, I'd like to know," Freda said. "It's an accident waiting to happen."

"I think it's a simple mistake. The hinges should have been set higher up the railing post and for some reason the gate was hung without the mistake being properly appreciated."

"The gate is in an out-of-the-way corner," Freda said. "Its only use that I can see is for someone to go down this ladder to replace the bulb in the light down there." She pointed to a large lamp intended to light the deck immediately below.

"Well, you can be sure the problem will be fixed soon," Pauline said, "which is why I wanted to see it again today."

"Now you've seen, let's get away. I feel creepy just being here."

"We have to get away quickly anyhow," Pauline replied, "because I can see our excursion boats being lowered into the sea and made ready. If we don't get to breakfast and dressed for hiking soon, we'll miss the excursion."

Later, when they were on the tender and heading for the island, Pauline said, "It's like they used to say about the army, everything is 'hurry up and wait'."

They'd gobbled down breakfast, raced to their cabins, dressed with lightning speed and then sat idly on the boat deck for fifteen minutes waiting to get a seat on a tender that would carry them to shore.

The tender docked and they stepped out to the newly built stone pier on an almost flat island covered in desert-like vegetation.

"We'll get scratched to death if the path hasn't been cleared through those cactus things," Freda said.

"We're explorers, Freddie. We don't care about stuff like that."

Freda's withering stare suggested Pauline was wrong.

Their guide gathered them around to explain why this

island was important and to remind them of Captain Ferguson's morning message.

"Normally," the guide said, "we only stay here for half a day. With the changes to our schedule, you'll have longer on the island if you wish to stay on after our hike."

He paused to see if that raised any questions and when it didn't, he continued, "This is the longer of the two walks so if you've changed your mind, or have gotten on the wrong boat, now's the time to say. The guide for the shorter hike will be here in the last tender, which I see making its way over from the ship. We can transfer you over to the shorter hike."

No one moved and he continued, "*Excelente*! You are all in the right place and ready to hike. Some background information before we leave: Some of the things we will see on this island include a subspecies of land iguanas, very unlike the marine iguanas you'll see throughout your cruise. Normally, you'd see this at the end of the trip and the contrast between these and what you would have been seeing up to this point would be more striking to you. This time, you'll have to hold the memory in mind to the next island in order to appreciate the contrast. Now, remember, these particular iguanas live only on this island. It was these small differences among the creatures of the islands that got Charles Darwin thinking about how species develop and, from that, how life on this planet developed. What we call nowadays the theory of evolution."

"As well, we will visit some cliffs on the other side of the island," he paused to let the groans from some of the party subside, before he continued with a grin, "Don't worry, it isn't a very big island. When we're there we'll see some of the spectacular seabirds that make the Galapagos Islands their home."

To Pauline, the iguanas looked very much like the iguanas they'd seen the day before on Santa Cruz. Iguanas she hadn't taken a lot of notice of because she'd been so focused on giant tortoises. The seabirds were more interesting for they included the darkly malevolent-looking frigate birds. Watching them swoop and soar overhead was fascinating, like seeing a pre-historic pterodactyl in flight.

"I thought the iguanas would be bigger," Freda said, as they watched a group of them sunning themselves on a rocky outcrop.

"Disappointed already, Freddie?"

"Not at all. It's just the tortoises were so unusual, not like we're used to, and I'd expected the iguanas to be something different too, I guess."

"Are we staying on the island after the hike is over?" Pauline asked.

Freda shook her head. "It's too hot for me," she said. "I should have acclimatized before I came on this cruise."

"The sun is hot," Pauline agreed, "but I find the air pleasant and the breeze even better."

"If it wasn't for the breeze, you would have been carrying me by now," Freda said. "For me, it's back to the ship, an excellent lunch and then some time in the shade."

"Tomorrow's first stop will be better for you because it isn't a walking trip," Pauline said. "It's a ride in one of those rubber boats they have hoisted up on the deck. You're not sure of the heat; I'm not sure about those rubber boats. The sea is pretty calm here, maybe that's why they got lulled into calling it 'pacific', but I'm used to seeing those little rubber things on lakes, not oceans."

"They're called Zephyrs, Polly, and they're perfectly safe. You see them on all the exploration documentaries."

"At least they'll keep us cooler than today's hike is doing," Pauline said, "which is what I was trying to say. We'll need swimsuits instead of sunhats."

. . .

THAT EVENING, Pauline, Somerville and Ferguson regrouped in the captain's cabin.

"I hope you enjoyed your first day on the islands?" Ferguson asked.

"Sure, sure," Somerville said. "More to the point, I learned our friend Jose had a run in with a passenger the day we boarded the ship."

"You refer to the misunderstanding with Mr. Weiss?"

"Call it what you like," Somerville said. "It wasn't mentioned before."

"Mr. Weiss misunderstood what Jose was doing with the baggage. The matter was easily settled and amicably," Ferguson said.

"You're speaking of Arvin Weiss? The man who shares our table at dinner?" Pauline asked.

"The very same," Somerville replied. "It isn't only bus drivers he takes exception to, it's guys carrying his bags, too."

"What an annoying man Mr. Weiss is."

"Agreed. But could his paranoia, you can hardly call it anything else, spill over into bodily harm?"

"I wouldn't have thought so," Pauline said. "However, as you say, people who see slights and persecution in everything, may lash out and cause harm."

"I'm sorry," Ferguson said, "what is this about bus drivers?"

Somerville explained the incidents at the start of the bus journey from Quito and how Arvin had characterized the exchange later that evening at dinner.

"Oh dear," Ferguson said. "I do hope a passenger isn't involved in this unfortunate incident."

"A passenger being responsible would be better than a crew member being responsible though, I would have thought," Pauline said.

"Yes, but the passenger will, in their own defense, claim

they were provoked by the crew member. Even if it isn't true, the mud will stick."

"Everyone on the bus and around the dinner table that night will be happy to give Mr. Weiss a 'character reference', Captain, I promise. I was ready to order the driver and tour guide to leave without him that morning and I was ready to blow a gasket at the table that evening," Somerville said.

Captain Ferguson smiled. "I hope it won't come to that. Mr. Weiss was perfectly happy when the true situation with the baggage was explained to him. I'm sure there was no lingering rancor."

"Maybe, but I'm going to question his movements that evening."

"I think the captain is right," Pauline said. "If Arvin had any grievance left, I'm sure we would have heard about it over dinner."

"You can assume that if you wish. Nevertheless, I'm going to question him, though maybe I'll do it informally first. You know, just two men shooting the breeze over a drink at the bar."

"Did you learn anything new when you spoke to my officers, Miss Riddell?" Captain Ferguson asked quickly, eager to change the subject.

"Officer LaPorte gave me the names of three other Peruvians among the maintenance and engineering crews. I'd like to speak to them in the coming days."

"You think Jose may have recognized one of them as a soldier or guerrilla and they killed him when he told them that?"

"I think it's possible or maybe some less horrific ancient grievance that got out of hand. I haven't lost sight of the possibility it could just be a scuffle that led to a tragic accident."

"I pray that is the answer if it isn't a straightforward accident."

From the briefing, Somerville led the way straight to the bar, Pauline following reluctantly behind. If Arvin was in the bar, she wanted to hear first-hand what he would say when Somerville questioned him.

"Hey, Arvin," Somerville said, placing his drink on the small table at which Arvin was sitting alone, "mind if we join you?"

Arvin waved his hand at the empty chairs indicating his agreement but noticeably failing to say anything.

"I hope you don't mind, Mr. Weiss," Pauline said, "but I'm sure you can understand why we'd like to talk to you."

"You want to pin that guy's death on me."

Pauline sighed. "No. We simply want to hear what happened when you saw the victim removing your bags from what you believed was your room."

"It was a mistake. What the hell? Haven't you guys ever made a mistake?"

"Of course," Somerville said, "only this happened after the bus incident and before the fall incident so you can see why we're asking you to tell us what happened."

Arvin's expression became grimmer than ever. "The bus has nothing to do with anything, that guy was hating on me. What happened to the dead guy later has nothing to do with the bus or my mistake over the bags. You're lumping them together to get me."

"We're really not, Mr. Weiss. Detective Somerville is just saying there were three incidents in one day and because two of them involved you," she held up her hand to stop him jumping in and continued quickly, "people may jump to the wrong conclusion. We need to be able to say that it is a wrong conclusion. Won't you help us do that?"

Arvin scowled but nodded.

"You were walking toward your cabin when you saw the victim leaving it with your hold-all bag. Is that correct?" Somerville said.

Arvin nodded.

Suppressing a sigh, Pauline said, "Why don't you continue?"

"What can I say? I saw the guy carrying my bag. I thought out from my room. I shouted. I realize now I was still upset from the coach ride but I really thought he was taking my bag."

"Only, it wasn't your room."

"That's right. My bag had been put in the cabin next door and the guy was just moving it to mine."

Arvin had stopped again. He was clearly uncomfortable about the event. Pauline wondered if indeed that might mean he was involved in Jose's death.

"And then?" Somerville said.

"He stood there grinning, saying 'yes' when I asked what he was doing. He had this big grin on his face and to me it looked like him saying 'come and get it if you want it'. I grabbed my bag and he let go. He was still grinning. After the bus driver's scowls all day, having this guy smirking at me was too much. I lost it and shoved him against the wall. That's all there was."

"One of the other crew who could speak English intervened and sorted it out, I understand," Pauline said.

"Yeah, exactly. When I realized, I apologized. Look, this was nothing. Just a hard day that led to a misunderstanding. Everybody was okay. I tipped the guy generously and we parted as friends."

"What about the evening?"

"What about it? I was on your table at dinner, don't you remember?"

"We do," Somerville said. "We remember you were the first to leave the table as well."

"I went to the bar. Everything that could go wrong that day had gone wrong and I was churning inside. I wanted a drink and an early night to settle my nerves, which is what I did."

"What time did you leave the bar?" Pauline asked.

"I don't know. Early. I didn't want to talk to anyone. I had a scotch. Drank it practically in one go and left."

"Did you speak to anyone at all?"

"No. I just said that."

"Very well," Pauline said. "Did you see anyone when you returned to your cabin? Anyone on the deck, in the corridor?"

"No. Everyone was still in the lounge, I guess. I told you. It was early, right after dinner."

"Is there anything you can tell us that might help?"

"No. I went to bed and slept. I didn't hear or see anything."

They thanked him and walked away. Outside, where there were few people around, Somerville said, "I can't stand that man, but I believe him."

"He's not a likeable man," Pauline agreed, "but I think a very lonely one."

"Maybe those two traits are related," Somerville said sarcastically.

Pauline smiled. "True. I'm going to keep an open mind about Mr. Weiss, though. He has no alibi for the evening and he's one of the very few people on this ship who doesn't."

8

ISABELA ISLAND, PUNTA VICENTE ROCA

THE MORNING'S ZEPHYR RIDE – the one Pauline had been so sarcastic about a day earlier – took them along the sides of the hopefully-now-extinct volcano's caldera and it was spectacular. Dramatic cliff faces soared towering above them as the boat slowly cruised the edge, nosing into vast sea-caves that echoed their voices. Even Pauline could feel herself caught up in the excitement of photographing the seals and turtles that swam around the boats. Fellow explorers with bigger cameras and zoom lenses were capturing pictures of nesting birds on the cliff face and seabirds high above, as they wheeled and swooped against the brilliant blue sky. It was a moment to remember.

As they returned along the cliff face, they saw their more adventurous fellow travelers snorkeling among the sharp up-thrust rocks, where the ever-present, garishly colorful Sally Lightfoot crabs scuttled about hoping for their next meal. Pauline and Freda weren't strong swimmers so just watching the snorkelers being lifted up by the sea onto rounded peaks of waves before sliding down into deep troughs of dark water made them feel queasy.

"I'm glad I wasn't tempted by that," Freda said, as a

particularly large swell lifted the boat and then sank it down. "It's bad enough in the boat."

"Maybe you don't feel it so much when you're actually moving with the water," Pauline said, with more hope than conviction.

"My plan is never to find out," Freda said. "That water looks black; the bottom is so far away."

"A bit how my brain feels, to be honest," Pauline said quietly. "I know we're looking at a murder but I don't yet see who or how."

"Oh, that," Freda said. "I'd forgotten."

* * *

"IT IS A LOVELY TEASHOP, isn't it?" Freda said, back onboard and looking around the corner of the ship's principal lounge area. "They make it very homey with just a few screens between the pillars. You'd never think it was one big open space really."

Pauline followed Freda's gaze. It was true. This open area was used in many different ways throughout the day on the ship. It was a small ship so space was at a premium.

"It is nicely done," Pauline agreed, "and I do love a teashop."

Freda sensed her sister wasn't as thrilled by the surroundings as she was. "You don't like it?"

"I like it," Pauline said. "They could hardly do better when there's no place for a cozy, separate room. But like everything in today's world, it's a facsimile of the real thing and that always makes me uncomfortable."

Freda nodded. "I know what you mean, but they mean well."

"I'm sure they do, dear," Pauline said, smiling. She looked again at the menu. Two pages of passionately described coffees and half a page of various exotic teas, none of which sounded particularly appealing. She sighed. A server approached and Pauline looked up.

"What can I help you with today?" the server asked.

"Hello again, Maria," Pauline said. "You have a busy time of it. Cleaning cabins in the mornings and serving in the ship's restaurants the rest of the day."

"We do many different things throughout the day," Maria said. "We have to. There's so much to do and we have quite a small staff."

"At least that must keep things interesting," Freda said.

"It does and I'm never bored. We're never without something to do," Maria replied. "I like that."

"I can imagine," Freda replied. "That's what I loved about nursing, in the beginning."

Pauline decided it was time to re-direct the conversation before Maria was given Freda's life history.

"I'd like English Breakfast tea, with milk, and one of those small macaroons I saw as we walked in."

Freda said she'd have the same and Maria left.

"Maria seems nice," Freda said.

"Their livelihoods depend on them being nice, Freda dear," Pauline said. "As do their tips."

"You've cruised before and become cynical," Freda said. "For me this is a new experience and having everyone we meet smiling and being pleasant is wonderful. It doesn't happen enough in life, in my experience anyway."

Pauline watched the others arriving to take the tables around them. They were uniformly old and plump, as the people were on the other cruises she'd taken. All the eating and drinking didn't bode well for their future health but maybe they were just doing what any sensible person would do at the end of their life – enjoy themselves. After all, she thought, no one gets out of here alive, as some sad pop singer had said not so long ago – before killing himself through the usual unpleasant lifestyle they imagined they were enjoying.

"You seem lost in thought," Freda said as Maria was returning with their pots of tea and pastries.

"I was a bit," Pauline said. "Murders always give me gloomy thoughts. But now we have tea to put all that right."

"Tea does soothe and calm, doesn't it?" Freda said, as she waited for Maria to place the many items she was carrying on her tray onto the table.

"It does and I think history proves it," Pauline said when Maria was gone.

"History?"

"Yes, history. It may sound a grand theory born out of a humble cuppa but our empire was created by coffee drinkers in the 1700s and ended with tea drinkers in the 1900s. Coffee makes people aggressive and energetic. Tea makes people calm and restful. You can't build or keep an empire by being calm and restful."

Freda laughed. "You were always the one for wild flights of fancy," she said.

"When some learned professor writes a book about it to great acclaim, before you're impressed by his great learning, remember you heard it first from me."

* * *

DURING LUNCH, while the ship sailed from Punta Vicente Roca to Fernandina Island, Captain Ferguson had invited the ship's three Peruvian crewmen to meet with the detectives. They sat in a semi-circle with their interpreter alongside staring impassively at Pauline and Somerville.

"So," Somerville said, after Captain Ferguson had asked them to outline their own personal histories as it related to the voyage, "none of you knew the victim before you joined the ship. But did you talk with him during your training?"

"I did," one of the men said.

"Me also," said a second. The third shook his head.

"Did he tell you anything about himself that might help us?" Pauline asked, and waited while the interpreter translated.

The men shook their heads.

"Nothing at all?" Somerville asked.

One of the two men began to speak. The translator said, "He said he was a refugee from the south and he'd had a horrible life."

"Are any of you from southern Peru?" Somerville asked.

When the translator had finished speaking, the men shook their heads. They spoke and Pauline could at least understand, "Lima."

"Did he say what had happened to him in his life that he was anxious about or anything in his present circumstances?" Pauline asked.

The men shook their heads when the translator put the question to them.

"Are any of you anxious in your present circumstances? After all, the events unfolding in your country right now are awful."

Again, the men shook their heads.

Pauline and Somerville glanced at each other.

"Gentlemen, thank you," Somerville said.

All four men filed out of the cabin and Somerville closed the door behind them.

"What did you think?" he asked.

"Maybe they were telling the truth," Pauline said, "but, I think there's something there and, as with Arvin, two of them can't provide an alibi."

"That's how I feel too," Somerville said. "They're

unlikely to have had anything to do with it but it's not impossible, or even improbable. We heard nothing that would conclusively rule them out."

"We need the company to find out if all three really do come from Lima and not the south. And we need to know if Jose spent time in Lima after escaping the south and leaving Peru. We can't just take these people's words."

"Agreed," Somerville said.

Captain Ferguson took down the information they required and had the questions radioed to the company's head office.

"On a happier note," Ferguson said, "did you enjoy this morning's excursion? Were you on the boat ride or the snorkeling?"

"I did the boat ride," Pauline said. "I didn't think I would enjoy it but I really did. I may even have some good photos. I hope so anyway. The guide told us our next stop, Fernandina, is an island of newly hardened lava rock. That sounds different."

"Yes, Fernandina is a barren place," Ferguson said. "There you'll see how all these islands began. Later, when you visit the other islands you'll see how life turns barren rock into habitable land. It's fascinating. The other, older, islands have a good covering of vegetation and even good soil. I visited here on a number of occasions during my years at sea. You know it was an old haunt of pirates and whalers before civilization caught up with the region."

"Our guides have told us," Pauline said, smiling. "I can't help feeling a bit nostalgic for those days when they talk about them."

"That's the romantic in all of us," Ferguson said. "Like dinosaurs, pirates seem attractive, lovable even, when they're extinct."

Listening to their conversation, Somerville was growing

impatient to leave. "I've one more person to interview," he said, heading for the door.

"Who would that be?" Ferguson asked but Somerville was gone.

"I don't know, Captain," Pauline said. "He never mentioned this until now."

"I fear he is torn between competing with you and collaborating with you, Miss Riddell."

"Oh dear. I hope not."

"And you? Have you any new thoughts on our incident?"

"Lots," Pauline said, "but I prefer to let them stay thoughts for now. Suspicion is a dangerous emotion once it's loose."

9

FERNANDINA ISLAND, PUNTA ESPINOZA

THE ZEPHYR BUMPED against the newly installed landing spot and the crewman threw a rope ashore where another crewman tied it quickly to a bollard. The zephyr was soon pulled close to the wave lashed platform where, of all people, Detective Somerville was assisting people to step out of the boat, which rose and fell dramatically in the swell.

"Miss Riddell," Somerville said, as he clasped Pauline's arm and steadied her, "welcome to Fernandina Island." Pauline gave him a tight, humorless smile in reply, before asking, "Why are you helping the rest of us ashore?"

"The guys were busy. They asked and I volunteered, and they said I looked strong enough." He laughed.

Pauline didn't like his laugh; it sounded triumphant, but she couldn't deny his strength was a comfort to the passengers as he brought them off the boat. When Somerville assisted Freda ashore, they made their way to where the naturalist guide was waiting.

"I feel seasick," Freda said. "I hope we won't be using those rubber boats at every island. They're okay when the sea is calm but horrible when it isn't."

"Sometimes they use the lifeboats as tenders. I don't

know how they decide when to use which," Pauline said. "The tour brochure only mentions wet or dry landings so it's either this or 'wet landings' which, I guess, means jumping into the sea at a beach. This was a dry one, according to the brochure."

Pauline looked about. The black lava that made up the only ground she could see was undulating and broken, with deep gullies and sharp cutting edges everywhere. It looked as she imagined a lunar landscape might. She was pleased she'd brought proper hiking boots for it would be easy to turn an ankle and anyone who fell here would be severely sliced and diced when they hit the ground.

Once the group were all gathered, the guide began to explain the geology that had brought this barren volcanic island into existence. As he spoke, Pauline saw Somerville making his way toward her. She kept her expression neutral, though her annoyance was intense.

"What have I missed?" Somerville asked.

"It's a volcanic island," Freda replied.

"I thought they all were," Somerville said.

"And you'll miss the rest if you don't listen," Pauline said in what she hoped was a quelling tone.

He grinned and turned to listen to the guide who was now describing the 'colonist' plants who began the process of occupying the barren rock and the vegetation that would come later when the 'colonists' had died and left enough nutrient for 'pioneer' plants to grow in. The guide went on to describe the iguanas and birds that lived here and those they might see today, and how some of them were used in Darwin's theories about evolution.

Somerville's impatience began to become obvious to people around him, as he fidgeted, twisted and turned, looking about for the highlights the guide was describing.

"You're very impatient, Mr. Somerville," Pauline said.

"I like to be busy. Can't stand waiting or just watching. I have to be doing."

"We'd noticed, but you came to see the islands and their fauna and flora," Freda said.

"I can see it just as well on the move. In fact, I think I'd see more."

The guide seemed to take the hint for he told them to follow him and not stray off the path; the ground was very uneven.

"Finally," Somerville said, loud enough to be heard by the whole party.

"You're eager to explore the island. That's good." Freda's tone suggested the opposite of good.

"I'm eager to get this tour done with and get back to the ship so I can start interviewing the crew," Somerville said, this time quietly enough to be only heard by Pauline and Freda. "Now we've got started on the investigation, I resent any interruption."

"What would you have done if this unfortunate death hadn't happened?"

Somerville grinned. "I guess I'd have zipped my lip and done the tours but now it has happened, I'm going to find it hard to do that."

Pauline shook her head. He may be an admirable young man in many ways but, in the end, he was a very young man and not one who she'd want investigating a possible murder. Experience and judgment were the qualities she'd have chosen. If there'd been a choice.

Their hike wasn't long, only difficult for many to navigate. The broken lava underfoot was treacherous, especially where wet. However, the party arrived safely at the rocks and beach that were their destination. The largest colony of marine iguanas in the Galapagos lived here, the guide said, and Pauline could believe it. They were piled one on top of another in writhing mounds of red and black scaly flesh. It looked most unappealing to Pauline. She presumed the iguanas liked it. Where the rocks were free of iguanas, there were sinister-looking cormorants drying their wings, which made no sense at all to Pauline for they were flightless birds. One of the many unusual adaptions found here on these islands.

* * *

THEIR DINNER TABLE that evening was silent. The other tables were made up of parties traveling together and they were all more cheerful and boisterous. The group on Pauline and Freda's table seemed to be those who knew no one and were consequently drawn together only by being excluded from every other table. She didn't know if that were really true but certainly they were always the same subdued eight.

Rod's expression was even grimmer than usual but tonight his sarcastic comments, if any, were kept to himself. His wife, perhaps depressed by his smoldering resentment, was almost equally quiet, her usual gaiety gone.

Arvin was still unhappy about being questioned the day before and his was an injured silence. Pauline thought that a good thing, on the whole, for you could never tell where his obsessions would take him, and them.

The Mennonite couple were never talkative but slowly, Freda was able to have them provide their views on the two islands they'd seen. For this, Pauline was grateful because she and Somerville were as silent as the others. The thoughts that filled their heads could not be shared at the table.

"Does your religion allow for evolution?" Pauline heard Freda ask. Pauline froze. Politics and religion didn't belong at the dinner table, that was the rule she'd heard from being a child and she still thought it good advice.

"We have not read Mr. Darwin's theory, so it is hard for us to comment, Mrs. Holman," Isaac said.

"But you have heard of it?"

"Oh, yes. In fact, I've brought his book *Origin of Species* to read as we explore the islands. From what we were told by our parents, and the Elders, it doesn't sound like it would be acceptable," Ruth said. "However, we are of a reformed group and we understand Darwin was a Christian who had his own struggles with what he was proposing. If he found a way to reconcile his theory with his beliefs, how can we say that we mightn't be able to do the same if we studied the subject."

"I heard it is about 'adaption' rather than 'evolution'," Betty said, suddenly joining in. "My Pastor says it doesn't disprove the Bible; it just explains how things changed over time after they were created."

Pauline heaved a silent sigh of relief. With luck, the conversation would continue along lines that wouldn't lead to yet another death. For her own part, she was struck by the way Rod occasionally glanced at Somerville. There was real anger in that. Was Rod the person Somerville had so mysteriously gone off to interview and, if so, why? What had he learned that had taken him off to question Rod without sharing the results with Pauline or the captain?

After their coffee, Pauline and Freda walked the deck under a clear sky filled with stars. There were other guests out but it was still quiet enough to talk privately.

"Did you notice Rod was even less communicative than usual tonight?" Pauline said.

"Yes. I think it was because he and Detective Somerville were arguing in the lounge earlier," Freda said.

"Ah, I thought it might be something like that."

"I tried to hear what they were saying but it wasn't easy. They were clearly upset but not shouting. In fact, their voices were lower than usual, I'd say. Particularly Somerville's."

"You heard nothing?"

"Rod said 'Mexican' once. I heard that."

"I wonder if he is Mexican. He's very tanned."

"Dark complexions always tan, and his coloring is very Spanish" Freda said, shrugging. "It doesn't mean he's from South or Central America." Freda and her husband had been on many Spanish holidays in recent years and she felt she knew enough to argue this point.

"I agree but he must have meant something. I wondered if Somerville had learned he was Latin American and asked if he was Peruvian, that's all."

Freda thought for a minute. "He does look Spanish, doesn't he? Very sexy, I think."

"You aren't planning to run off with a bullfighter, I hope."

Freda smiled. "I might, you know. I don't hold with cruelty to animals but when Keith and I went to Spain on our holidays, those bullfighters did catch my eye. In the world today, we don't see such courage displayed with so much elegance. I have to admit I was smitten." Her expression grew troubled. "I feel guilty about that now that Keith is gone, to be honest."

"You couldn't know Keith was going to die so soon and it was only a thought, not a deed. You have no reason to feel any such thing."

"I know but strange memories come back. Usually, they're good memories but occasionally there are some I don't like to recall. It seems we often harbor unkind thoughts and they haunt us when we least expect it."

"I wonder when it will be safe for me to interview Rod," Pauline said, thoughtfully, hardly noticing Freda's wistfulness.

. . .

"WHAT DOES the company know about Jose?" Pauline asked Captain Ferguson when they met to discuss progress.

"I was sure you would ask this question," Ferguson said, with a smile. "I asked them to translate and send the interview and background checks that were done." He handed a sheaf of papers to Pauline and Somerville.

They read them quickly.

Pauline said, "Well, it says little more than what we've been told. Jose was a refugee from Peru living in Ecuador."

Ferguson nodded. "I spoke to our personnel manager, the one who approved the hiring of most of the technical crew. He said Jose's story was a horrific one and he filled in some additional details for me. Jose was captured by the Shining Path guerillas on his way to school on the morning of the massacre. They forced him to take part in the massacre, not by actually killing people but in telling them information about the villagers. He was so scared that, when the killing began and he saw the guerillas weren't watching him anymore, he escaped into the forest. He followed trails that eventually led him over the border. He didn't even know he'd made it to Ecuador at first. He was so in fear of his life, he'd avoided everyone as he traveled. It was only when he'd become ill that he went into a town and begged for help, which is when he discovered he was in another country and was safe."

"It sounds like we have to consider the real possibility that the guerrillas caught up with him on this ship," Somerville said.

"Then the murderer," Pauline paused as she saw Somerville frown, and then continued, "if there is a murderer, is one of the crew and not a passenger. However, how did the guerillas know he was here? His story, if true, sounds to me like the guerillas *aren't* our suspects."

"I think it most likely to be a member of the crew anyway,

don't you?" Ferguson said. "The passengers only arrived here hours before the voyage began. They hardly had time to discover Jose existed, let alone work up enough anger to kill him. And, as you say, how would the guerillas know and why would they care if some kid spoke about them? They live out in the wild and care nothing for the law."

"One or two of the American passengers are Latin American," Somerville said, thinking out loud. "They could have had family who knew about Jose and they might blame Jose for helping the guerillas."

"We should consider that," Pauline said, "but it's more likely to be a crew member, as Captain Ferguson suggests."

"We need the same information we have on Jose, Captain," Somerville said, waving the papers to indicate what he wanted, "on all the crew. Certainly, the male crew members."

"It takes time for the fax machine to print out that much information," Ferguson said, "but I'll have them start right away. You think only a man could have sent Jose over the railing?"

"I'm sure of it," Somerville said. 'He wasn't a small or weak man."

"Miss Riddell?" Ferguson asked.

"I agree, Captain. It's unlikely to be a woman," Pauline said. "Not impossible, though, so we shouldn't completely rule out the female crew members."

"Anything else?" Ferguson asked.

"Yes. I'd like to speak to the head of personnel," Pauline said. "Could you arrange for us to interview him by radio?"

"I'm sure that could be arranged," Ferguson said. "I'll contact our head office right after we finish here and set it up for tomorrow night. That way you can enjoy your island excursions and Mr. Hidalgo, our local Ecuadorean recruiter, can gather the information you want to discuss."

10

ISABELA ISLAND, URBINA BAY

THEY'D BEEN WARNED by the guides that this site was a 'wet landing' and they'd taken that to mean they'd get wet feet. It was way more than that. By the time everyone was ashore, using the demonstrated 'park your butt on the side and swing your legs over' method, everyone's clothes were soaked. The unsteadiness of the elderly passengers, the boat with its nose on the sand, its tail bobbing about in the inrushing waves, all contributed to most people getting a dousing. Many simply slipped off the wet sides, lost their footing in the sea and were swallowed up by the surf. Some fell backward into the boat, were caught by the guide, and maneuvered over the side, where they were invariably unready for the waves that splashed up and soaked them. If she hadn't been so embarrassed at her own lack of agility, Pauline would have paid money to buy a movie of this first interesting event.

"Still, the water is refreshing," Freda said, wringing out her sunhat, which had blown into the sea as she'd slithered over the slippery, rubbery sides of the boat.

Pauline laughed. "And it makes the trip more memorable. I actually feel like a real explorer now."

The walk soon dried them off, which led to a new source of irritation as the salt water dried on their skin and in their clothes. In the heat, salty itching made them feel like they were being bitten by the clouds of flying insects.

"'May be hot' the excursion guide said," Freda grumbled, as the bushes crowded in on them, blocking even the merest hint of a breeze they'd enjoyed on the beach. "This isn't hot, it's baking."

"When you live in England," Pauline said, "everywhere else on the planet seems hot."

"Not Norway," Freda replied. "Keith and I went there five years ago in August. It was like our October, so cold and wet."

"That's probably why the Vikings left," Pauline said as she made her way carefully across the ridged volcanic rock. "Some of the older folk are going to struggle here," she said, staring at the trail ahead of them.

"Most of the older people are on the shorter hike."

"You said Betty was. That would please Rod." Pauline grinned at the thought of the grim, taciturn Rod assisting his wife over these broken boulders and razor-sharp ripples of solidified lava.

They followed the guide and listened with half their attention as he told them the seahorse-shaped island was actually five volcano cones that had merged together to form a single island. He said the volcanoes were still considered to be active and they all laughed politely when he suggested one may erupt today and bring additional excitement to their visit.

The walk took them among deep pools fringed by brilliant green vegetation, so different to the 'colonist' plants on the newly formed Fernandina. Finches flitted among the bushes and cameras clicked and whirred as the keenest members of the party tried to get that great photo to show their friends and neighbors the amazing sights they'd seen. Pauline, whose opinion of the utterly nondescript birds wasn't high, couldn't help thinking the friends and neighbors would likely be unimpressed.

The afternoon was to be another long hike at a more southerly part of the island. When they'd planned this trip, she and Freda had agreed that it would be great having all day off the ship, walking among the flora and fauna of the most unusual islands known to man. Now Pauline was wishing she'd planned to stay onboard and read a book. This first hike felt like more than enough to satisfy her needs.

The walk, however, did have something to interest Pauline. Set back from the shoreline, which, according to their guide, had been raised more than twelve feet by an earthquake back in 1954 was the remains of a coral reef, now marooned inland. For the first time, Pauline got a sense of just how unstable these islands were and how precarious was the existence of their birds and animals.

The hike, too, got better as the morning wore on. Because the older and slower people had chosen the optional excursion, this hike kept a good pace that felt exhilarating after trailing around at the speed of giant tortoises as they'd done the day before. It also brought her into contact with Ruth and Isaac for the first time away from the other dinner guests.

"Hello," Pauline said, "are you enjoying this fast hike too? I'm pleased to be moving again instead of dawdling along."

"We are indeed enjoying it," Isaac said. "We're working people, so a vacation is something strange for us and today feels more natural."

Pauline nodded. She could see both of them working in the fields. They had the stocky, strong frames of farmers.

"Can I ask you about the night of the accident?"

"It will make a change from questions about whether we've lost our faith now we've seen the light of Darwinism,"

Isaac said, with again that hint of humor she'd seen so often in him when answering impertinent questions about their beliefs.

"I imagine," Pauline said. "You left the lounge after dinner so you might have heard or seen something in the quiet of the outside. Did you?"

Ruth said simply, "No."

Isaac added, "We have thought about this, and repeatedly walked through that evening in our minds. We were outside. The evening was so beautiful but then it grew dark and the wind was cold. We returned to our cabin to read. Everything we saw made sense then and still does. We saw officers on the bridge and heard people talking in normal voices, not raised in argument. The voices we heard, we didn't recognize."

"That's disappointing," Pauline said. "Do you remember what time it was when you left the dinner table or arrived in your cabin?"

"Not really," Ruth said. "Time doesn't mean as much to us as it seems to mean to you folk."

"It's true. We're obsessed with it, aren't we?"

"As with so much else we find puzzling," Isaac said. "Do any of these things you all crave and pine for make any of you happy?"

"Now, you're teasing me," Pauline said. "I'm sure you know the answer as well as I do. But I think it's as the American Constitution says, it's the 'pursuit of happiness' and not the 'achieving happiness' that makes all our lives meaningful."

Isaac smiled. "We don't have much to do with the U.S. or any other national constitution, but it does describe life correctly – the pursuit of happiness. It's how people pursue it that differs, I guess."

Pauline was about to reply in kind, when she stopped.

"You said people talking in normal voices. Can you say more about that?"

"What is there to say? There seemed to be people outside on the decks, maybe balconies, talking. They didn't sound angry or frightened."

"Were they speaking English or Spanish?"

"English."

"Did they have an accent?"

"Everyone has an accent," Isaac said, "and all of your accents sound strange to us. But if what you're asking is 'were they crew members', I think the answer is no. They were passengers."

"Men or women?"

"Men," Ruth said.

"Two or more?"

"There were two groups of men, I think," Isaac said, looking to Ruth for confirmation. She nodded.

"More than two in each group do you think?"

"Possibly but probably just two pairs of men, outside smoking and talking," Isaac said.

"You were on the lounge deck. Were they out of sight on the same deck or above, on upper decks?"

"One group was above us on an upper deck. The other, I think, the same deck but around the other side. That's how it seemed anyhow. As I said, ordinary. Nothing that would suggest violence."

"That's good to know. Now, if we can find those people, they may have heard something that you didn't."

Pedro called a halt and the group gathered around him. "We rest here for five minutes, no more," he said. "Drink lots of water because we will be out in the sun for the return trip and it is very hot."

One of the more argumentative passengers pounced on Ruth and Isaac. Pauline, though sorry for the young couple, took her chance and left them to their fate. She moved quickly over to where Freda was waiting.

"Did you learn anything?" Freda asked as Pauline joined her.

"Yes. There were others on deck that night."

"No one has mentioned being there."

"No, they haven't so we need to find out who, when, and why they haven't mentioned it."

"That's easy," Freda said. "No one has asked them. You and Somerville have been busy asking questions of the very few people you suspect. If I wasn't being asked, I wouldn't volunteer any information either."

Pauline smiled. "I thought you were an upright, honest citizen," she said.

"I thought so too," Freda admitted, "until I realized this is serious and bad things happen to simple people who get caught up in serious things."

"Still regretting volunteering to help detect, Freddie," Pauline said, grinning.

"I honestly don't know why you choose to do this. One day someone will kill you. You do know that, don't you?"

Pauline's expression changed to one of long ago and far away. She shook herself and replied, "A long time ago, my friend Poppy said I was a soldier in the war against injustice. At the time, it seemed over the top. I was just trying to find out why another friend had been murdered. The words have stayed with me, though, and I think they explain it best. I may be killed one day, as you say, but it will be in a just cause and what more can anyone ask for in the end?"

"A quiet 'going to sleep' in my own bed with my family around me," Freda snapped. "And that feels quite unlikely right now."

"I don't have a family," Pauline said. "Now, when we get back, circulate and start asking questions. We need to find the men on deck that evening and learn what they heard and saw."

When they returned to the landing site, they found many of those who had taken the short, slower walk were already snorkeling around the rocks that formed the breakwater.

Pauline and Freda liked the look of the calm shallow waters of the small bay. After the heat on the hike, they thought a swim would be perfect. They both took the offered goggles and snorkel.

Pedro had told them the water on this side of the island was cold because of the peculiar way currents lifted water from the deep to the surface. For the sisters, used to bathing in the North Sea off Yorkshire's coast, they found it warm but still refreshing and nothing like the harsh waters they were used to. Underwater, colorful fish and rays swam by, along with what looked like small torpedoes that they knew were actually penguins, the only penguins to live this far north – and only because the cold water made it possible. An occasional shark sailed across their vision, which was unnerving. If they hadn't been told they were nurse sharks and harmless, they would have left the water vertically like cartoon characters and not stopped paddling air until they reached the beach.

* * *

BACK ONBOARD, Pauline was met by the security officer, Sanchez, and escorted to the Captain's cabin where she found Somerville had already arrived.

"I have Señor Hidalgo on the radio, Miss Riddell," Captain Ferguson said. "I felt it would be good for you and Detective Somerville to meet him, even if it has to be at a distance. This way you can ask directly what information you're looking for."

Mr. Hidalgo fortunately spoke excellent English, so

Pauline and Somerville were able to ask questions and receive answers that required no interpretation or explanation.

"In your mind," Pauline asked, in conclusion, "the checks you did confirmed Jose was a genuine refugee and the other members of the crew from this part of the world are highly unlikely to be linked to any of the various factions fighting for control in Peru?"

"That is correct," Hidalgo said. "We have to be very careful with our hiring here, as you can imagine. There are many different political groups who have the support of many people. We did extensive checks on all of them."

Somerville asked, "You say there was no evidence Jose took part in violence but can you really be sure? He admitted to leading the guerillas who'd captured him to the village where he'd lived. That alone must be suspicious."

"We thought of all that, Detective, but remember, he was little more than a child when he was taken by them and they assured him they had the best intentions in going to the village. Their mission, they said, was to help and support the people. He was traumatized by what happened."

"You say a child but this was less than two years ago," Pauline said. "He was just twenty when he died and therefore around eighteen or nineteen when it happened. I don't consider nineteen a child. I suspect many of the guerrilla band were much the same age."

"Nevertheless," Hidalgo said, "our intensive review of his life and known behavior convinced us it would be wrong to decide against him. And, after all, it is he who was the victim here, assuming there was any wrongdoing."

"The point is, his behavior in the past may have led to his death," Somerville said.

"All the evidence says he was a victim then and maybe he is a victim again." Hidalgo paused, and then added, "Have you considered suicide? Could it not be that his experiences preyed on his mind until he could no longer stand it?"

"That may account for the superficial cut under his chin," Ferguson added. "If he'd initially tried to kill himself with a knife and then found he couldn't do it."

Pauline shook her head. "The cut was under his chin, not on his throat. Even the most reluctant of suicides would know the difference. And if it was suicide, there is a vast ocean just one step off the rail. No, this wasn't suicide."

"I don't think we should dismiss the possibility too quickly," Somerville said. "Who knows what goes through the mind of a person at these low moments."

"And none of the others among the crew were found to have any connection to the village where the massacre Jose mentioned took place, or a connection to Jose himself?" Pauline asked Hidalgo, ignoring the suicide discussion that was continuing between her two companions.

"We weren't looking for such a connection when we screened the interviewees," Hidalgo replied. "I have asked the police here to do that now. It may take a day or so for them to complete their research."

"We look forward to hearing the results of those investigations, Mr. Hidalgo," Somerville said. "I have nothing more to ask tonight but would ask that you be available to answer questions about details in the faxes you're sending. I hope that can be possible?"

"Certainly," Hidalgo said. "If Captain Ferguson can make the radio link available, I'll be happy to respond to anything you have to say."

Ferguson replied, "Miss Riddell, Detective Somerville, and I meet each evening to discuss their progress. I'll have the radio operator make it possible for you join us."

* * *

TO FILL IN THE TIME, as the ship sailed along the coast of Isabela Island to its next stop, the regular superb lunch was replaced by an even more sumptuous barbecue.

Pauline and Freda each took small plates of lobster, steak and salad up to the next deck to escape the crowd. Their stratagem, designed to protect their tightening waistbands, backfired. When Maria saw them escaping, she made it her job to supply them with everything on the menu, far more than they could ever manage. By the time the meal was over, they could barely move.

"Thank you, Maria, but we have another hike in an hour," Freda said, despairingly, when the server had offered yet more dessert or an after-dinner port. "We couldn't possible manage another mouthful."

"Señora," Maria replied, tut-tutting sadly, "you will walk it off and be hungry."

Freda shook her head but, smiling, she said, "Our guides Pedro and Raul will have to carry us back, more like."

"Working together they couldn't lift me now," Pauline added.

"We're doomed," Freda said, when Maria left them, clearly disappointed in their capacity to consume. "We'll sink the zephyr when we step aboard."

"Us and everyone else," Pauline said. "Taking one passenger per zephyr will be the only safe way."

11

ISABELLA ISLAND, PUNTA MORENO

ALTHOUGH THE ZEPHYR was pulled up tightly to the rocky ledge of the dock, and they could step ashore without wading in the sea, the landing was again far from a 'dry' one. The stiff breeze that had plagued them in the morning was also bringing waves splashing over the landing stage and making the boat rise and fall rapidly. Even with a strong man onshore to grasp the passengers and haul them from the boat and onto the wet, smooth, volcanic rocks, the disembarkation got them soaked.

They'd picked their excursions when booking the cruise and Pauline and Freda had chosen the longest hikes at each stop because Freda intended to see everything she could in the time available. Many who had been on the morning hike had decided to take it easy in the afternoon, so it was with a smaller band of only the hardier souls that they set out into the hinterland. The breeze that had made landing so hazardous, and they'd hoped would cool them as they hiked, was lost the moment they left the open area of lava rock and entered low bushes that covered the slopes of the volcano's side. The bushes soon gave way to a landscape of dark pools of brackish water fringed by vibrant jungle-green plants that stood out in stark contrast with everything they'd seen up until this time.

The guide stopped frequently for water breaks and to point out the occasional wildlife, usually a small dark-colored bird flitting among the bushes. In Pauline's eyes, they were all indistinguishable from half the birds she saw at home. A hawk soared above them at one point, a Galapagos Hawk, the guide said. It too looked just like any other hawk to Pauline.

The rest of the group, however, seemed happy enough, if the clicking of camera shutters was anything to judge by. For herself, Pauline felt she would never go on another nature vacation as long as she lived. Not even an African safari with guaranteed lions could tempt her at this moment. The march seemed to stretch out before her, an undulating, sharply pointed, rocky wasteland of time.

"You're not as excited as the rest of us, Pauline."

Pauline thought Freda sounded a little bit angry. "I'm taking everything in and storing it away for future memory," Pauline said. "You can be sure of that."

"Good, because this is one of the most significant places on Earth."

"I know, Freddie. I'm not completely clueless," Pauline said. She was though. Absolutely clueless – when it came to Jose's death.

LATER, back on board and resting in Freda's cabin, Pauline said, "I had a few minutes quiet time to speak some more with Pedro. He says he saw a man arguing with Jose later that afternoon, just before dinner was served. It's possible he only says this now, when he must know we're suspicious of him, to deflect our attention from him to someone else, but we must follow it up. He thinks it was Rod Chalmers, and from the description he gave, I think it was too."

"Maybe this is what Somerville heard and why he had that interview he never shared with you or the captain."

Pauline said, "We need to get Rod on his own. I don't know how, but we must."

"Shouldn't you interview him with Somerville? It might make Somerville confess to having already interviewed Rod."

"Somerville is like a bull in a china shop," Pauline said. "A man like Rod will not respond well to the detective's style. I think we'll do better without him."

"But you will tell him, won't you?" Freda asked. "The last thing we need is a feud with Somerville – or the captain deciding you're untrustworthy."

"I'll tell them tonight, don't worry. Then it will be too late for Somerville to pounce on Rod before we can."

* * *

"THE FAXES you sent on Pedro Morales," Somerville said, speaking loudly for the radio connection was fading, "I think there's something wrong about Pedro."

Hidalgo's voice crackled over the faltering connection. "It's true. The information we had when we hired him was that he was from Lima. The police have found that isn't exactly true."

Somerville snorted. "It's barely true at all. He was born there, lived there until he was six but then lived the next twelve years in the village where Jose lived and which Jose betrayed, before returning to Lima only two years ago."

"Yes," Hidalgo said unhappily. "There may well have been a connection. Not that it would have changed our view of hiring him. Pedro had returned to Lima before the massacre and we had no reason to assume he knew or had a grudge against Jose. And we still don't," he added but even the static couldn't hide the concern in his voice.

"Nor do we, Señor Hidalgo," Pauline said. "It is just another puzzle. For a young man so apparently unconnected with anyone here, Jose seems to have been remarkably linked to many others. Pedro is the third person we've discovered with a possible link to Jose."

"The other two were just angry incidents," Somerville said. "This is deeper and, to my mind, has far more potential."

"Possibly," Pauline said, "but Jose is the only person on this ship to have two angry incidents in the very first afternoon. No one else had any. Jose seemed to invite or maybe just attract problems."

"I feel we may have gotten a good lead, at last, and your theory may not be as wild as I'd first imagined, Miss Riddell."

Pauline smiled. "You taking me seriously means a lot to me, Detective," she said.

Somerville reddened. "You know what I mean," he said. "I wasn't being snarky."

"Nor was I," Pauline replied.

"Captain," Somerville said, abruptly changing direction, "I think we need to talk to Pedro Morales right away. Tonight. I don't think we should wait."

"I'll have him found and brought here," Captain Ferguson said, lifting the phone.

PEDRO WAS CLEARLY UNEASY. He twisted in the chair they'd placed before them and viewed the three, Ferguson, Pauline, and Somerville, with what looked like alarm.

"We aren't the police, Pedro," Captain Ferguson said. "We've just learned that you once lived in the village where Jose lived, though before the people were massacred. We hoped you might have known Jose or known something about him that would help us get to the bottom of this mystery."

He paused, hoping the crewman would begin to speak. When he didn't, Ferguson asked, "Did you know Jose before you and he joined the ship?"

"No, and I didn't live in the same village. My father was schoolteacher at a village higher up the mountain. We were about five kilometers from where Jose said he lived."

"So, did Jose say where he came from?" Pauline asked.

"Yes. He spoke more than once of the horrors he'd seen and his escape. He thought we should treat him differently because of what had happened to him. Personally, I think he boasted about what had happened."

"I would have thought a refugee would want to forget the past," Pauline said.

Pedro nodded. "I, and others, thought it strange as well."

"He was a young man," Somerville said. "While being afraid for his life at the time, after, he possibly thought it exciting and expected others to think so too. Did others think so?"

Pedro shook his head. "I think most who met him among the crew thought him foolish and a…" he struggled for a word.

"A braggart?" Pauline offered.

Pedro frowned. "I don't know that word. Do you know *machismo*?"

The others nodded.

"Well," Pedro said, "like that but without any reason for it. He was not a manly man and his machismo was false. I can't explain better."

"You didn't like him?" Somerville asked.

"No, sir, I did not."

"Was it only his wrongly assumed machismo or was there more?" Pauline asked.

Pedro shrugged. "I didn't know him until we met the crew. I am a naturalist and not one of the technical or hospitality crew. I don't say he picked a quarrel with me during the training, but it felt like he did. He made unpleasant comments about me to others, in my hearing."

"Why was that?" Ferguson asked, "And why didn't you alert one of the ship's officers?"

Pedro's expression turned even more sullen. "I didn't know him, but he learned my father was a schoolteacher in the nearby village to his and I was a university graduate. Those two facts seemed to be enough for him to hate me. Those are the reasons he gave anyway."

"But this dislike never led to violence, did it?" Pauline asked.

Pedro hesitated, and then said, "One evening, after the training sessions had ended for the day, he pushed me against a wall and punched me, trying to get me to retaliate. I didn't. It made him even more contemptuous than before. I avoided him as much as I could after that."

"There's nothing in any of what you remember of your life near the village where Jose lived that could help us understand what happened to him?" Somerville asked.

"Nothing except I understand why it happened to him and not to someone else."

"Then you think it was murder?" Pauline asked.

"Do not put words in my mouth," Pedro said. "I only say I can understand why he might meet a violent end when others didn't. I know nothing of murder."

Ferguson looked at the two investigators and, seeing no further questions coming, said, "Thank you for being so honest with us, Pedro. It must have been very difficult for you."

When Pedro had left the cabin, Ferguson asked, "Did any of this help you, Miss Riddell, Mr. Somerville?"

"I think we need to know a lot more about Pedro and what has been happening among the crew," Somerville said. "He may have been honest, but he may be holding back something that could blow this case apart."

"I agree we need to interview more crew members to get a better understanding," Pauline said. "And I think Pedro does believe Jose was murdered, but I shall wait until we know more before I decide whether this is a defining moment in the case."

"There's one other thing I learned from Pedro earlier today," Pauline said and quickly outlined the information Pedro had given.

Somerville was excited. "I knew it," he said. "That Rod guy's as crooked as they come. I shouldn't say this, but Betty needs to be alive to her surroundings or someday she'll find she isn't alive at all."

"Detective Somerville," Ferguson said. "In this room, we may speak plainly, of course, but you must not say such things outside here."

Somerville grinned. "Don't you worry, Captain, I can keep my mouth shut when I need to. But this information is what we need to sweat that guy a bit. What do you say, Miss Riddell?"

"Certainly, we should interview him, Detective, but I'm not the sort who 'sweats' people. I find talking to witnesses works just as well."

"Maybe in those middle-class dramas you involve yourself in but in the real world there are people who would find talking to old ladies a hoot. They'd play up to them, telling them whatever they want to hear. They're pretty damn good at being all things to all people."

"Nevertheless, Detective, I insist, when we talk to him, we do so in a civilized manner."

"Well, sure, ma'am. We'll be as sweet as candy. On my honor."

Pauline was not convinced by this profession of good behavior and was more than ever determined to get to Rod before Somerville. Overnight, she had to come up with a plan.

12

MORNING AT SEA

AS IT HAPPENED, she didn't need to do anything, for Rod did something they would never have suspected of him, though perhaps they should have expected because he was a fitness instructor before he married. Nevertheless, they were surprised when he turned up for the ship's exercise class at six am the next morning.

As they met him making his way up the stairs on the way to the class, Pauline asked, "I wondered if we might talk privately for a moment, Rod, after the class?"

"What about?"

"About Jose," Pauline said.

"I've already told that detective all I know, which is nothing. And I've told him twice. If you're going to the class, I'm leaving."

This announcement about Somerville so angered Pauline she was momentarily speechless. Fortunately, Freda was able to step into the breach.

"Please don't do that," Freda said, quickly. "We aren't out to trap you. Just understand."

They reached the highest deck, where the center was brightly lit, the instructor already waiting.

"My regulars are here, I see. Welcome back, ladies," she said, with a beaming smile, "and welcome to a new face too, sir."

Rod's dark expression seemed even more sinister in the shadows on the edge of the lighted circle but his nodded reply was friendly enough.

All three took up station by one of the mats laid out on the deck. The instructor always laid out six mats but in the three days Pauline had attended, today was the first time there were more attendees than just her and Freda.

The best part of the class, to Pauline anyway, was while they stretched, the sun rose swiftly over a new island each morning. Today was no different. Darkness gave way to a purplish haze in the shadows created by the low mountain, until the island's features, indistinct at first, were laid bare in the bright sunshine. Today's island was a dry, dun-colored hill rising out of the sea, lightly covered in scrub vegetation like so many of the islands they'd seen. It was no wonder that, at first, people had thought of them as 'the land that time forgot'. They looked ancient and primeval, as did the creatures that lived on them. It took a Darwin to recognize they were exactly the opposite of that.

The moment they left the class, Pauline took up her earlier question with Rod. "Someone mentioned seeing you having a quarrel with Jose. What was that about?"

"The detective asked me the same thing. I'll tell you what I told him. I didn't have a quarrel with Jose and even if I had, it would still be no business of yours."

"We're only trying to set the cruise company's mind at rest," Freda said. "They just want to be sure it was an accident."

"Well, I can't help you there so if you'll excuse me, this is where I leave you," Rod said, gesturing to the door that led to the first-class suites.

When he'd gone, Pauline said, "I'd hoped if we got to him first, we might do better with a woman's touch."

Freda grinned. "I think he's off women right now. Marrying for money hasn't been as painless as he imagined, I think."

"Hush, Freddie. We don't know he married for money."

"If that's how your detecting mind works, Polly, I'm not surprised it takes you forever to get the right answer. Men marry young women for children and old women for money. You don't need to be a detective to work that out."

"That doesn't mean there can't be love, or at least affection, involved," Pauline said primly.

"Well Rod's affection evaporated quickly 'cos he's been as cross as a bear with a sore head since this honeymoon cruise began." Freda paused, and then added, "How does one know if a bear has a sore head, I wonder?"

"I expect it's when they're cross, Freddie, and you're right about Rod. If I'd expected a suspicious death of anyone on this ship, Betty would have been the victim and Rod would be the chief suspect."

"But it isn't Betty. The thing is, though," Freda said, "we could easily believe Rod had killed Betty because he seems exactly the kind of man who would kill someone, which is why it's so easy to believe he killed Jose."

"And he doesn't want to say why he was quarreling with Jose – if he was quarrelling with Jose."

"Do you doubt it?" Freda asked.

"Only one person claims to have seen him and that's Pedro, who also had a history with Jose that we've only just discovered. He only announced he'd seen Rod quarrelling with Jose after we began questioning him," Pauline reminded her.

"Oh, yes. That's true. I hadn't thought of it like that. So, Rod, who looks like an elegant movie villain, may be telling the truth and Pedro, who looks like a nature-loving choirboy, may be leading us astray."

"Possibly," Pauline said. "But to get a better idea about that, we need someone else who saw this quarrel."

"Do you think it was Rod and Jose talking that Isaac and Ruth heard?" Freda asked.

Pauline shook her head. "It can't have been. According to Pedro, Rod was arguing with Jose in the late afternoon. Isaac and Ruth heard people after dinner when it was dark."

"I think we should confirm with Pedro what he remembered," Freda said. "It could be just different words, afternoon and evening, for the same time. We have to be sure."

"Well, you're my detecting partner," Pauline said. "You check with him. I feel I'm wearing out my welcome there."

"YOU WERE RIGHT," Freda said, as she rejoined Pauline in the lounge after talking to Pedro. "It was still light when Pedro saw Jose arguing with Rod."

"There must have been other people about," Pauline said.

"Don't forget, it would be the time the afternoon excursion came back on board. People would all be down on the rear deck meeting their friends and enjoying the champagne we're constantly being plied with on our return."

"True but not everyone," Pauline said. "We were there and the deck wasn't so very full. Not nearly everybody aboard was there and not even for the free champagne. A lot of people were elsewhere on the ship and someone should have seen this exchange, if it happened."

"We can't question all the passengers."

"Nor can we broadcast a request to the whole ship," Pauline said. "It's very unsatisfactory, this way of investigating."

Freda laughed. "You didn't realize how much help you usually get from the police, did you?"

"To be honest, I did know," Pauline said ruefully, "but, as you say, haven't appreciated it enough until now. They can do things we amateur sleuths can't do."

"We can ask questions of everyone," Freda said.

"You're really getting into this, aren't you?" Pauline said, smiling.

"I am. Maybe, now I've stopped working, I'll be a detective too. I'll pick up your mantle back in the Old Country."

"Just don't advertise using my name or I'll sue," Pauline said, and then added with a grin, "You see how much I've learned since I came to North America?"

"Actually," Freda said, suddenly serious, "I'm thinking of going back to nursing. I retired because Keith's health had forced him to retire early. There doesn't seem much point now, does there?"

Pauline hugged her sister briefly. "Don't rush into anything. Give yourself time."

"First we have to discover 'who dunnit' here on this ship," Freda said. "Who are our suspects?"

"Number one has to be Pedro," Pauline said, "and for all the reasons we've talked about. Number two is Rod, he's strangely reticent about his whereabouts at the time of Jose's death and won't give a satisfactory answer to the question about the argument with Jose. If it happened. Number three, for me, is Arvin..." She held up her hand to stop the objection she could see Freda about to make. "You can tell me why you don't think Pedro did it when you tell me who you think did it," Pauline said. "And number four is Mr., or should I say, Señor X, one of the crew we haven't yet unmasked. Someone who knew Josc from before and had a reason to kill him. Now, you can tell me who you think 'dunnit'."

"I think it has to be your Señor X because I don't believe anyone we've spoken to is murderer material."

Pauline grinned. "What you're saying is you want all the patients to get well."

"Of course, I do. Who wouldn't? But I have a sensible reason for saying this. It isn't just well-wishing."

"And what's that?"

"None of the people we've spoken to have known Jose long enough to want to kill him. Don't you think?"

"It's true they don't have any good reason that we've discovered and the short acquaintance would normally suggest they're unlikely suspects but Jose seems to be the kind of person trouble gravitated to. I'm not convinced of the passengers' innocence yet."

"What do suggest?"

"What you said, we ask questions of everyone we meet, and as quickly as we can," Pauline replied. "We can start right now in the lounge tonight and continue at breakfast in the morning."

* * *

AS FREDA happily chatted to the passengers in the lounge, Pauline excused herself saying she would be back in a few minutes. She quickly made her way down to the deck where the guest relations and other offices were.

She was fortunate because the woman she'd come to see was behind the desk looking bored.

"Good evening, Nina," Pauline said. "Can I ask you some questions?"

"I'm here to assist guests," Nina said.

"As you know, I'm helping the captain confirm that awful tragedy really was an accident," Pauline said. "We, Detective Somerville and I, have questioned many of the male crew members. We feel it more likely that, if Jose was helped over the railing in any way, it would have to be by a man. He was a strong young man himself."

"I too think that is most likely," Nina said guardedly.

"However, I wondered if you'd heard anything among the female crew members that might help us?"

Nina shook her head. "No," she said. "I don't think any of us knew him. We're all very new onboard, you know."

"I understand," Pauline said. "If you do hear of anything, I hope you'll let me know. I can be very discreet."

"I can be very discreet too, Miss Riddell," Nina said.

Pauline had hoped a woman-to-woman approach would lower the barriers between them but decided it would take more than that in the case of someone who grew up behind the Iron Curtain. She nodded and returned to the lounge. A different approach was going to be needed to hear the female side of the crew's story.

* * *

OVERNIGHT, new information from the mainland had arrived and Ferguson called the two detectives early to his cabin for them to review it while Hidalgo was available to talk. One piece in particular caught Pauline's attention.

"Señor Hidalgo," she said, "this newspaper article about the school soccer team and it's triumph in Lima suggests Pedro almost certainly traveled to the village where Jose lived. Do we have anything that says if Jose was on his school's team or maybe a village team that could have brought him and Pedro into contact?"

"We haven't anything like that at this time," Hidalgo's reply crackled over the radio making him hard to understand.

"We must find out," Somerville said loudly, as though volume would make the radio reception better.

"I'd already thought of it and they're working on that."

"It really is beginning to look as if Pedro had an earlier relationship with Jose and he might be our man," Somerville said. "I don't say murderer but involved in the incident, quite likely."

"I hope not," Ferguson said. "He's one of the nicest young men on board: helpful, kind, and hard-working. I'd be sorry to find he has a hand in this."

"It's early days, Captain," Pauline said. "Jose may not have played soccer and never met Pedro. It may not be likely, but it's possible."

"Every boy and man here in South America plays soccer, Miss Riddell, as I'm sure you know. It's inconceivable Jose didn't."

"Captain Ferguson is right," Hidalgo said. "Another batch of newspaper articles is on its way right now. We've just received one that says Jose played for his school and his village soccer teams and would almost certainly have played against Pedro at some time."

"This is growing more serious," Ferguson said. "Pedro didn't tell us this."

"We still don't know they actually met, Captain," Somerville said. "I play hockey and baseball, have done all my life. I barely knew the people on the teams I was on at school, let alone the players on the other teams."

"But this isn't Toronto, Detective," Pauline said. "These are two small villages not three miles apart, and in a region where people must travel to meet each other. Very like the one where I grew up, in fact. You may not have known your neighbors in the city, but I knew people from miles away because they were family, schoolfriends, or others we met in school and village events. There's much wider interaction when there are much fewer people nearby."

"Still," Somerville said, "we need Pedro to explain

himself. If he says he didn't meet Jose while they were each on separate soccer teams, then we're not a lot further forward."

"I think we're closing in on something like a conclusion," Ferguson said, "and I don't like it at all."

"Understandable." Pauline said. "We need to question Pedro again to arrive at the truth of this."

"I'll have him found and brought here right away," Ferguson said. "If there's any chance this is something more than an accident, I want it known now."

The three continued discussing the latest information sent from shore and relaying yet more requests for information to Hidalgo while they waited for Pedro to arrive.

"Ah, Pedro, come in," Ferguson said, when the young naturalist knocked and requested permission to enter. "Please take a seat. We have more questions to ask."

Pedro was barely settled before Somerville said, "How is it you failed to mention you and Jose both played on your school and village soccer teams and you must have met at some time?"

Pedro was taken aback by this sudden attack by his inquisitors.

"I didn't mention playing on the local soccer teams because you didn't ask me," Pedro said. "I knew how it would look to you."

"It looks even worse now we've discovered it," Ferguson said, "and know that you withheld this information."

"I didn't know Jose before we arrived on this ship," Pedro said, "but I did recognize him and him me when we arrived."

"We asked exactly that and you said you didn't know him," Pauline said. "That makes us very suspicious of you, as I'm sure you can appreciate."

"Of course," Pedro said, "but I thought it best not to let you waste your time on this because it has nothing to do with his death. I was evasive, it's true, but for good reasons. I didn't kill him and the hate he harbored toward me wasn't behind his death."

"Why did he dislike you?"

"For the reasons I gave and because I was something of a sports star at school. Our soccer team went to the capital and won a trophy and he didn't. These were the reasons he gave while trying to intimidate me. They are petty, childish things. Things we all harbor about something or someone in our past but eventually the rest of us grow out of it. He didn't. I was just unlucky enough to run into him again and he was able to vent his resentment."

"You have no alibi for the time in question; the victim had a grudge against you; he'd already threatened you once. You can see how it looks," Somerville said.

"None of which condemns me," Pedro said, suddenly sitting up and becoming very firm in his bearing. "I repeat, you are wasting your time on this wrong road. If you decide to take this further, I will produce a solid, clear alibi for the time in question. Until then, you must accept my word. You are wrong. Look elsewhere. Now, unless you have anything else to ask, I'm leading a hike this morning and will return to my work."

The three inquisitors were so taken aback by this transformation from evasive youth to stolid adult, they were stunned for a moment.

"I have no more questions," Pauline said.

"I have many, but I'll leave them for now," Somerville growled.

"You may go, Pedro," Ferguson said, "but you and I need to talk later."

When the naturalist had left the room, Somerville said, "He did something."

Pauline said, "But not, I think, what we feared."

"You think he was with one of the passengers, Miss Riddell?" Ferguson asked.

Pauline nodded. "Which is, I'm sure, against company policy and could have him fired. However, admitting it, if he has to, is better than being arrested on suspicion of causing someone's death."

"He's a fast worker then," Somerville said. "We'd only just gotten onboard."

"Well," Pauline said, "he's a very attractive boy."

'But you like a more mature man, do you, Miss Riddell?"

"I no longer give the matter any thought, Detective. Now, how do we proceed with our remaining suspects?"

* * *

ALONE IN HER CABIN, and dressing automatically for the morning's hike, Pauline stared out of the porthole and thought. Pedro had been the most likely of the obvious suspects, but his words had convinced her of his innocence. For him to make such a statement, with all that it entailed, said he really was innocent of murder. She would not demand he produce his alibi, nor would she encourage Somerville or Ferguson to do so either. Some things were best left unsaid and private.

Where did that leave her? Squashed, is where she was – in the middle of the road and squished flat. She had been that sure it was Pedro. Her disappointment was intense. Her belief in herself unraveled and doubts, always crowding in, took possession of her mind.

What was so odd about this case, and had been causing her much unease, was how much it resembled her first case. Then, as now, everyone was happy with the official verdict and only she saw a different answer. Like that first time, it was she, Pauline, pushing others to find a murderer that others thought didn't exist. Since that time, most of the mysteries she'd solved had been her working with others as they reached the right conclusion, even if they hadn't always agreed at the start who was the guilty party. They had all been working to establish the truth. This felt like her career had come full circle and, more than that, was drawing to a natural close.

Was that the path her life was intended to follow in future? Was this fate, God even, giving her an opportunity to call an end to the strange 'career' she'd had? Maybe it was her subconscious. People nowadays were very hot on their subconscious. Was it telling her that a new country required a new start and a casting off of her old life?

That was the bigger picture but what of the smaller, more immediate problem? If not Pedro, then Rod, Arvin or Señor X, the mystery suspect who she'd suggested earlier but who never appeared. X would certainly be one of the crew, but they all seemed to be just regular people.

Hidalgo was still searching, of course, and something may appear but probably not before the ship docked back on the mainland. That only left the other two. The first, Rod, seemed hugely unlikely, whatever a real or imagined quarrel with Jose might suggest. That left the morose, sad Arvin. Poor man. Unable to shake off the monsters in his past, did he lash out and unwittingly cause Jose's death? If he did, his own anguished spirit would haunt him until his dying day. It seemed unfair to burden him further.

Wishing she'd kept to her original refusal to take part, Pauline sighed, left her cabin and knocked on Freda's cabin door.

13

FLOREANA ISLAND, POST OFFICE BAY

AS THEY WERE LEAVING their rooms on the way to breakfast, they wished Maria, waiting in the corridor to start cleaning, a good morning. She smiled and replied with her usual happy smile.

They were about to walk away when Freda said, "Maria, did you know Jose?"

The beaming smile on Maria's face disappeared at once. "He was a bad man," she said.

"Oh, did you know him?"

Maria shook her head. "He tried it on with me first day here on this ship – that is how you say it?"

"Yes, that's what people say. Did he molest you?"

"What is molest?" Maria asked, suspiciously.

"Interfered with you," Freda said.

Maria nodded. Her white teeth bit her lower lip and her eyes filled with tears.

"I'm sorry," Freda said, "I didn't know. It must have been horrible. Did you report what happened?"

Maria shook her head.

"You should, you know."

"He's dead now," Maria said. "The other men are good people. We don't need the trouble it will bring."

"I see what you mean," Freda said. "But how did you hope to keep him at bay throughout the whole voyage?"

Maria's expression hardened. "I meant to avoid him but now I don't have to. Now, please excuse me, I must get on with my work." She opened the nearest cabin door and stepped inside, closing the door quickly behind her.

"I wish I hadn't said anything now," Freda said. 'Poor Maria. How awful."

"You did the right thing," Pauline said. "I'll make a detective out of you before this case is over."

"It caused her so much distress. I bet she's in there crying her eyes out."

"Probably but she has given me a new possible motive," Pauline said.

"You mean Maria killed him?" Freda asked incredulously.

"Possibly, but more likely she told one or more of the male crew members and they decided to warn Jose off. I think someone may have been too energetic with the warning."

"It would have to be one of the men who particularly liked Maria, I think," Freda said.

"Or someone in authority, or someone who thinks they have authority. There are many possibilities, but we need to find out who."

"That opens the field of suspects up considerably," Freda said. "We can't possibly do all of it in what's left of the cruise."

"This line of enquiry will be simpler than looking for links to Jose's past," Pauline reminded her. "Everybody involved is still here on the ship."

"It also opens up another possible line of enquiry," Freda

said, slowly. "What if Maria wasn't the only woman he molested?"

Pauline grimaced. "We need to know who, among the women crew members, would be most likely confided in," she said. "I'd hoped Nina, who we met that night, would tell me if there were any rumors among the female crew but she wouldn't. We can't interview all of the female crew, any more than we could interview all the men."

"How can one man have caused so much grief in so few days?" Freda said. "I'm beginning to think that, if he was killed, as you say, the killer did us all a favor."

"Now, Freda," Pauline said. "You can't think like that. Everyone deserves a fair hearing and a just outcome."

They boarded the tender for shore and prepared for another day of seeing wonders that, in Pauline's eyes, weren't very wondrous. She still wasn't warming to this trip. If it wasn't for Jose's death, she'd have described the whole trip as 'murder'.

As they made their way down to the boat deck. Freda nudged Pauline. "Do you see who's here," she whispered.

Pauline had also seen Betty, without her husband, at the same time Freda had. "I see," she replied. "Why don't you go and say hello while I gather up the items we're supposed to take." For today's excursion, insect repellant was recommended as well as the obligatory hats and water.

Freda nodded and went off to accost Betty while the coast was clear.

Pauline gathered up extra bottles of water for them both and the snorkeling equipment they were to use if they decided to take part in the post-hike swimming. As she did so, she watched Freda make her way to Betty's side, and also watched the steps down to the embarkation deck from the cabin decks above, in case Rod made a late appearance.

He didn't but it was only when they were boarding the tender that Freda signaled Pauline to join her.

"Rod isn't coming," she said, as Pauline came closer, "so I've suggested we three keep each other company on the trail."

The three women joined the line and boarded the tender together.

"Your husband is sitting this one out, Betty?" Pauline asked, as they wedged themselves onto the narrow seats. The tenders were the ship's lifeboats and the thought of being crushed into one of these boats, perhaps for days before help arrived, made Pauline fervently hope their ship stayed afloat.

"He says if he sees another effing iguana he won't be responsible for his actions," Betty said, sadly. "I fear he doesn't appreciate the significance of all this. Really, he's just obliging me being here. I was the one who wanted to come."

Freda grinned. "We have the same difficulty," she said. "I'm fascinated; Pauline is keeping me company."

Pauline gave Freda a withering look but said to Betty, "It was good of Rod to do that, when he so clearly finds the experience tedious."

She tried to keep the sarcasm out of her voice that she felt must be obvious and continued, "My limited experience of men is their only interest in wildlife is as meat or targets so it must be boring to see wildlife that are neither."

Betty nodded. "Exactly," she said. "If he could have brought his gun, it would have been different. Though he says these creatures would make poor sport."

"They certainly would," Freda said. "You can walk up and pet most of them."

The tender bumping against the dock, and being tied alongside, interrupted the conversation while the crew helped the visitors step off the boat onto the shore.

Once ashore, Pauline took the opportunity of the group not yet being assembled to ask some sensible questions.

"Did Rod tell you what he was arguing with Jose about? You must have wondered."

"People have been saying that he and Jose argued but Rod never mentioned it to me and when I asked, he said it wasn't true. It was just people picking on him because he was Latin American."

"Well hearing he hadn't quarreled with Jose would be a relief, I'm sure. It must have set your mind at rest."

"It did, does, though it makes me angry the way people point fingers if you aren't part of the in-group."

"Don't I know it," Pauline said, laughing. "You can't believe the things I've heard said about my spinsterhood over the years."

"I knew you would understand," Betty said. "being single and never marrying, so I hear."

"We folks on the fringe have to stick together," Pauline said, smiling. "I'm thinking of forming a union."

"I didn't realize, until I met Rod, how difficult it can be to fit in with everyone sometimes."

"Does Rod feel it very badly?"

Betty nodded. "Men are brutal to each other, aren't they? If you're one of them, you can answer back in the same fashion, but if you're not you can't and you get frustrated by not being able to take part or even defend yourself. That's what Rod says anyhow."

WATCHING A DIFFERENT NATURALIST JOINING THEM, Pauline was relieved to see Pedro wasn't to be their group's guide and quietly said so to Freda.

"Do you really still think Pedro had anything to do with

it?" Freda asked, when they were moving off and they had some privacy.

"I've no idea," Pauline said. "I just feel it would be better if we weren't alone with him until this mystery is cleared up."

"But he's such a nice young man," Freda said.

"They wouldn't have been hired if they weren't nice people, Freddie," Pauline said patiently, though she was growing exasperated at her sister's constant Pollyanna view of people.

"But still," Freda said, "he's not the sort. Just look at him. He'd be no match for Jose and he'd avoid him not fight him."

"What if he couldn't avoid him? What if Jose backed him into a corner? What if Jose got in his face and Pedro pushed him away, only to see Jose topple over the rail to his death? What would a nice boy who avoids trouble do then?"

"They would get help," Freda said.

"Some would, others, once they were sure they hadn't been seen, would avoid trouble by getting themselves well away and saying nothing."

"Well, I don't believe Pedro would be one of those," Freda said.

Fortunately for Pauline's patience, the group had stopped to listen to the guide and they were now caught up to them. Further discussion of detection would have to wait.

The hike took them through the still visible foundations of old buildings and roads to the 'Post Office', which was a barrel where letters had been deposited by sailors for other sailors to carry home and post. This service had begun in the 1790s, the guide told them, and still continues today, though the cards left now are written by visitors and taken home to post by other visitors.

The group happily spent the next 30 minutes sifting through the many cards in the barrel, hoping to find one to carry home and post for a fellow countryman or woman.

Freda found two that were addressed to people in England and took them both.

Pauline was relieved to find all the Canadian ones gone by the time she was handed the bundles of cards remaining to be posted. Posting cards for people she didn't know, to people she didn't know, on top of the hours spent looking at empty nesting sites or indistinguishable birds wasn't as enthralling as she'd hoped it might be. In her mind, Darwin's famous finches all looked like small brown or black birds that only a naturalist or birdwatcher could tell apart – and she was neither. Some days it was relief to return to the ship and the next meal. She could only hope Freda, whose 'treat' this was, was finding it all she hoped for.

* * *

"I THINK everyone is taking a nap after this morning's hike," Freda said, back on the ship and looking around the almost empty lounge and coffee shop.

"One of the pleasures of having older people as fellow passengers is the quiet times where you get the nicest parts of the ship to yourself."

"It also means we can talk without being overheard," Freda said, checking to see the wait staff were well out of hearing.

"We can do that in our cabins," Pauline reminded her.

"It's not as nice as enjoying an afternoon tea and treat in this beautiful little teashop."

"True. Now, what did you learn about Rod from Betty. You had a good long chat when we were out there."

"Not a lot. She's sure Rod didn't hurt Jose but doesn't know where he was at the time. I think Rod's constant sulking is beginning to get her down though. He was supposed to be on today's excursion and then at the last minute refused to go."

"That's good news. If she gets angry enough she may tell us something revealing, instead of the loyal wife routine she's been keeping up."

"That's an awful thing to say, Polly."

"True but I'm more concerned with catching a murderer than being nice."

"What were you thinking of while you sent me off to grill Betty?"

"I was thinking about the cut under Jose's chin. I'd thought the cut was caused by a knife," Pauline said, "but now I see alternatives everywhere. I saw it first with a ring like the one Betty was wearing last night at dinner. It had sharply cut stones. I thought a necklace such as that one over there," she pointed to a woman just entering at the farther side of the lounge whose necklace had a large cross with sharply pointed ends, "or even something as mundane as the metal spring at the top of a clipboard."

"A clipboard?" Freda said. "Who has a clipboard?" She looked about the room.

Pauline smiled. "No one here," she said, "but didn't you see that steward this morning, checking off items as he inspected the pool deck?"

"I didn't notice."

"If you hope to become a great mystery-solver, you'll need to take notice."

"I didn't think we were worrying about that cut now," Freda said.

"Anything strange has to be part of the solution, even if we can't yet see how."

"You wouldn't threaten someone with a clipboard though, would you?" Freda said.

"But if someone closed in on you quickly, and you had a

clipboard in your hands at the time, you may thrust it up toward their head to try and ward them off. The metal clip could easily lodge under your assailant's chin."

"I suppose," Freda said, slowly, "but I don't see how it helps."

"It suggests to me that we've been focused on Jose and his past background when it really could be a very new quarrel with one of the crew who does regular checks of the equipment. Maria's information this morning seems very important taken in that light."

"This man wouldn't go to meet Jose with a clipboard though, Polly," Freda said.

"He could have met Jose earlier, had the discussion with others in attendance, and then Jose took an opportunity when the man was on his own, making checks on the ship with a clipboard, to confront him."

"All you're saying, Polly, is you have no idea who, or how, or with what, Jose was killed and that being so, it is just as likely to be an accident – as Detective Somerville says."

"Freddie, dear, we're still in the gathering evidence stage of the investigation. It's too soon to throw up our hands and give in."

Freda shook her head in dismay. "I'm going to have a nap before this afternoon's excursion," she said. "You might want to take the time to think, instead of daydream."

"Dreaming, or imagining, is what I do best," Pauline said. "And I think you're right. Some time to think would be good."

She'd no sooner placed her head on the pillow when the bedside phone rang. Pauline picked it up and said, "Yes."

"Good morning, Miss Riddell. Detective Somerville is with me and I felt we needed you here if we're to talk shop."

"I'll be there in two minutes," Pauline said, leaping from

the bed and hurrying to dress. She was at his cabin in less time than she'd predicted.

"Have you any progress to report?" Captain Ferguson asked, as he handed them their drinks. The briefings were becoming too much like a 'drinks with the captain' event in Pauline's mind.

"I've been following up on your chief engineer, Captain," Somerville said. "I think there's a good chance he was involved. I'm not saying he murdered Jose because I don't think anyone did, but I do think he backed the kid into a corner and the kid fell. An accident, nothing like that was supposed to happen but still not exactly innocent either."

Ferguson's expression hardened but he only turned to Pauline and said, "Miss Riddell?"

"I'm nowhere near thinking of naming a suspect at this time, Captain, but I've been making more enquiries about Rod Chalmers and Arvin Weiss, so far without any new evidence on either."

"But you are still sure it was murder, Miss Riddell? Or are you perhaps saying it's looking more like an accident?"

"Oh no. I'm sure Jose was killed. Detective Somerville's suggestion that Jose was backed into that corner and fell is possible and if so it may be manslaughter rather than murder, but it wasn't an accident."

"Why, though?"

"Because that corner is, so far as I and your safety inspectors could see, the only place on the ship where what happened, could have happened. If Jose was backed into there, it was by someone who knew that gate was low and loose."

"It has been repaired, by the way," Ferguson said. "The work was finally finished off when everyone was ashore today."

"That is good to hear," Pauline said. "Even roped off it was a hazard to anyone up there in rough seas."

"Quite!" Ferguson said, eager to change the subject. "Now, what are your plans to further your investigations?"

"I'd like more information on the chief engineer, if you can provide it quickly, Señor Hidalgo?" Somerville asked, addressing the personnel manager who was listening in by radio.

"And I would like anything more you can provide on Rod Chalmers, Arvin Weiss and Jose Garcia himself," Pauline added.

"The police are researching for us," Hidalgo said, "but they are slow. They have many more pressing priorities, as they never fail to remind us. You must understand, in their minds this case is closed."

"Have you no other avenues to call on?" Pauline asked.

"We work with a number of agencies who provide us with work candidates. They are looking into it but they have limited resources," Hidalgo replied. "In fact, the police are their chief source of information for personal backgrounds. With regard to the passengers, we can only go through the police and the embassies and they are understandably wary of revealing information to people who have no authority."

"Do what you can," Ferguson said. "We understand these aren't ideal conditions for investigating possible crimes."

"While we wait, Captain," Pauline said, "I'd like to ask for your advice on who might be the best person among the female crew members to interview. I know that up to now, we've worked on the assumption that whoever sent Jose over that gate must have been as strong or stronger than Jose. However, it's possible he was overconfident and then easily overbalanced by the slightest of pushes. A woman could have done that. We shouldn't neglect that line of enquiry."

"Very well, Miss Riddell," Ferguson said, "I'll ask our

hospitality manager, Suzanne, to answer your questions but I feel we're clutching at straws here."

"I agree, Captain," Somerville said. "I feel the more we eliminate people, the more people Miss Riddell will try to draw into the net." He glared at Pauline as he spoke.

"We haven't really eliminated anyone yet," Pauline said. "And, I find, we've been somewhat blind in our thinking. This new avenue may lead us to the truth."

Somerville shook his head in despair.

14

FLOREANA ISLAND, CORMORANT POINT

"YOUR HUSBAND ISN'T JOINING us this afternoon?" Pedro asked Betty, as he helped her off the ship and into the tender.

"He doesn't feel well enough to join us," Betty said, in an icy voice.

"Too much carousing last night," a man already seated in the tender called out. He laughed; others tittered quietly. Some mutterings suggested the carousing had continued this morning.

Betty sat, staring straight ahead, ignoring them.

Freda sat beside her and Pauline sat beside Freda. The tender moved off and the conversation grew as people recounted what the naturalist had told them to look out for and what they hoped to see. Pauline once again thought kindly of Rod's sarcastic comment about iguanas and stayed silent.

Another wet landing but by now Pauline and Freda were used to getting in and out of the zephyr as it bobbed under their behinds.

Once ashore, the group began forming into its small cliques, which very nicely left Betty to Pauline and Freda and the Mennonite couple who somehow never seemed to find their way into any of the different groups, being neither smokers, gamblers, nor pool nor bar people.

Hoping to give Freda more opportunity to get fresh information from Betty, Pauline led Ruth and Isaac to expand on their hopes for the day. The ploy seemed to work, she and the young couple followed a little way behind the main group while Freda and Betty trailed along at the back. Pauline could barely contain her impatience, surely this new letdown by Rod would tip Betty over the edge and she'd give something away.

Pedro stopped and waited for them to gather around before starting his narration. Pauline found it hard to concentrate because the expression on Freda's face said she had something to impart that would please her sister. Pauline nodded as surreptitiously as she could. She hoped that now the walls were down, they may learn much more to their advantage.

The walk too was uneventful, apart from the wasps that bugged them the moment they left the shore. Fortunately, the insect repellant they wore almost every time they set foot on an island seemed to keep the things from alighting and stinging anyone.

The island really was one of the most pleasant in the archipelago. Remains of old roads and homes with their gardens could be seen among the undergrowth. It was strange to think people had come here, settled, and lived comfortably for decades, centuries even, before abandoning the island when the capital was moved to Santa Cruz and the National Park established.

After their walk, easier on this most hospitable island, they snorkeled in the warm waters of the bay. An idyllic morning that Pauline found rather flat. Uninspiring was her opinion as she floated in the water looking up into the eternally clear blue sky. She had no new thoughts on the case and time was running out.

"You're very quiet," Freda said, rejoining her sister as she lay floating in the water.

"I'm letting my subconscious work its magic," Pauline said, not entirely satirically. She really was hoping something would strike a chord.

"Do you want to hear what I learned?" Freda asked.

Pauline tried to look around, realized that couldn't be done floating on her back and struggled to a more upright position treading water. Other swimmers were close, too close for safe discussion.

"Later, Freddie," she said. "When we're alone."

"Then I'll leave you to your musings," Freda replied, "before I drive them all away."

"They've had long enough and haven't delivered," Pauline said, resetting her goggles over her eyes and rolling to once again study the undersea life that swam below them. They paddled slowly across the rocky seabed, pointing out highlights to each other, letting the time drift away with the tide.

As she and Freda dried themselves and dressed to return to the boat, Pauline said, "We still haven't found the men who were on deck that night."

"I'm not sure they exist," Freda replied. "Arvin didn't hear them and Rod doesn't mention them. The only ones who heard them were Ruth and Isaac. Don't you think that odd?"

"Maybe," Pauline said. "It may just be the timing but why would they even mention it if it didn't happen? I don't think Mennonites are naturally dishonest or mischievous people."

"No, or natural murderers either."

"I have to say, you might have something there, Freddie," Pauline said. "What if they aren't Mennonites?"

"Not Mennonites? Why would anyone dress and present themselves that way if they weren't?"

"I don't know," Pauline said. "It's just that many times when they've been speaking to others, I've felt that Isaac, particularly, is laughing at us all. I thought it was because he sees us as unenlightened souls and, consequently, little more than children but what if it's because they're playing a prank on us all?"

"But why?"

"How should I know? A bet with friends back home? A whim?"

"Nonsense, Polly. You're losing your touch, if not your actual mind."

"That's possible too," Pauline said. "This is a puzzling case."

"Probably because it isn't actually a case."

Pauline sighed. "You still have doubts, Freddie? I hope they aren't preventing you from chatting in a meaningful way with our fellow guests."

"It's because I'm chatting with them my doubts are growing and so is the resistance I'm meeting when I ask a question on the subject. Aren't you finding that too?"

"There's always distrust when people ask questions," Pauline said. "You have to understand people don't want to be involved and to make that happen they say as little as they can."

"Well, you do some questioning when we get back to the boat and see if what I'm saying isn't true."

"It maybe because you haven't an official appointment to question people the way I have," Pauline said, "but I will continue questioning people and see if you're right."

Pauline's opportunity to ask questions came sooner than even she could have hoped for, shortly after dressing and before the tenders arrived to take those wishing to return to the ship, she found herself alone with Ruth. Isaac was talking to a man farther along the beach.

"Do you find these birds and animals as fascinating as many seem to?" Pauline asked, while she was pushing her wet towel and bathing cap into her bag.

Ruth shook her head. "No," she said. "They're all God's creatures and made as he intended them. I don't say Darwin was wrong, only that adapting to suit your environment isn't so big a change and suggesting it leads to new species, well, I leave that to others to argue about."

"I just find the differences too minute to see," Pauline said, "which leaves me lost. It's an odd thing for me to admit to as I usually pride myself on seeing what others don't."

"But small differences are huge, aren't they," Ruth said. "Tiny differences in doctrine leads to so much religious and social strife because it changes everything."

"That's very true," Pauline agreed. "In fact, I think, the smaller the disagreement, the larger the quarrel is often the case."

"We," Ruth said, hesitantly, "have powerful evidence of that in our own lives. My parents have quite cast us off because of Isaac's radical notions. This trip will certainly mean they will shun me forever."

"Yet you still came on it."

"Yes. You must follow your own truth in the world, don't you think?" Ruth asked. "This isn't a childish rebellion Isaac and I are on, Miss Riddell. It's a determination to bring some of the good things of the modern world into our world, without destroying what is good in our world."

"I do think we have to follow our own truth, however hard that is," Pauline agreed. "I've been puzzled to explain your presence on the cruise, to be honest with you, and now I think I understand."

"You will think us odd, I dare say," Ruth said. "We look

different, but you should understand that you people have always looked and seemed odd to us. We're trying to overcome our suspicions about you and bridge that gap for our children and those who come after."

Pauline smiled. "I've often thought Isaac finds us amusing. There's often a twinkle of laughter in his eye and his voice when he speaks to us. Does he find us very silly?"

Ruth laughed. The first time Pauline had heard her laugh. "He does find outsiders silly," she said, "but he isn't really laughing at you. Please believe me. It's just sometimes he hears himself telling the story to our people back home and imagining their reaction. You see, even though it is Isaac leading our small group to a closer understanding of your world, he still finds it hard sometimes to take your world seriously. None of you seem to show true reverence for the lives you've been given."

"I feel that way sometimes too," Pauline said. "Even I put my spiritual beliefs into a compartment so I can work and investigate when it should be those things that are in boxes."

"I think that's why we feel safer talking to you, Miss Riddell," Ruth said. "And probably why people tell you things they wouldn't tell others. They feel you will do what is right."

"I try to but it is often hard knowing what is right and what is not."

"Sadly, what is right and what is fun to do are often at opposite ends of the teeter-totter, don't you find?"

Pauline nodded but was saved from replying with the excursion party once again forming around Pedro to hear more about the Galapagos and its unique environment.

Her conversation with the usually uncommunicative Ruth had, for a time, taken Pauline's mind off the pressing desire to hear what Freda had learned from Betty. But the moment they were back on the ship, she grabbed her sister by the arm and practically marched her past the welcome aboard champagne and back to their cabins.

"I want to freshen up before we eat, Freddie," she said, when Freda protested.

"Well," Pauline demanded, once they were safely out of hearing, "tell me what you learned."

"Rod is a fool," Freda said. "He married money and only days after the wedding is throwing it all away."

"I don't care if Rod is the world's greatest court jester, Freddie. What did Betty say about that evening?"

"Oh, that," Freda said with a shrug. "Ow! Don't pinch! All right, all right. He wasn't with Betty as she's said until now. She doesn't know where he was and," she paused for dramatic effect, "he did have an argument with Jose."

"What about?"

"Jose was trying to extort money from Rod."

"To do that, Jose must have known of some wrongdoing on Rod's part. Does Betty know what?"

"If she does, she isn't saying yet," Freda said. "Maybe, if Rod hasn't come to his senses today and doesn't behave better tonight, she'll tell me tomorrow."

"Then here's hoping he's too far gone to care," Pauline said.

"And I hope not. I feel horrible for Betty."

"She must have been out of her mind to marry him," Pauline said flatly. "She could have had what she wanted by keeping him as a bit on the side. If people behave foolishly, they deserve what they get."

"Pauline," Freda cried, shocked to the core.

"Sorry, Freddie, but you know I'm right. Even if you won't admit it."

"I'm not going to be your spy tomorrow," Freda said, icily. "I've had enough."

"You're not my spy, you're my detecting partner so stop this nonsense and get on with your work."

"I will never work for you again."

"Think of all the fun you'll miss," Pauline said.

"It's not very nice, doing this."

"We're all different, I suppose," Pauline said. "You find snooping on people not nice, I find it infinitely preferable to changing bedpans."

"You carry on then, Pauline. I think you'll discover people really have had enough."

"Oh dear," Pauline said, grimacing. "I've been reduced to 'Pauline' have I?"

"Until you come to your senses," Freda replied, smiling. "And if you don't look out, you'll be Miss Riddell!"

Pauline laughed. She was still chuckling when she went in search of witnesses. Someone who would admit to being on the deck at the time of Jose's death. She found Freda was right. In the past day, the passengers' mood had changed. Many wouldn't even speak to her and those that did communicate, didn't tell her about their movements. Many were happy to tell her where her movements should take her. It seemed the mystery's novelty had worn off.

When they met for tea later that afternoon, Freda lost no time in asking, "Do you see what I mean now? People are tired of us endlessly badgering them with questions. They can't be comfortable with me or you or even each other, while we're trying to turn them into snitches."

"I do understand," Pauline said. "But *you* must understand, I've been doing this for years. You develop a thick skin eventually."

"It's all right for you. While you and Somerville are carousing with the captain, I'm in the lounge with the other folks on the outside and these past days I've been hearing a lot of opinions about this investigation and the detectives.

That's why I have to stop. I'm handing in my notice, Pauline."

Pauline nodded. "That's wise, I think. They can't take it out on me or Somerville because we were asked to investigate but you are in a strange position. For your own peace of mind, we should make it clear you're no longer a part of this – and by your choice."

"I've already done that," Freda said. "Everyone I talked to today, I told them I'm not taking part anymore. They were pleased to hear it. It means I can converse with them like a normal human being."

Pauline laughed. "I think you'll need time to win their trust after the past week or so," she said.

Freda grinned. "You're right," she said, "but, Polly, I'll never imagine your life of solving puzzles as being exciting and romantic again. I'm cured of that."

"Back to nursing it is, then?"

Freda nodded. "Yes, I think so. A world where we want everyone to go home free from hurt is the life for me. Even if we can't always make that happen."

Pauline was about to respond when officer Sanchez arrived at their table.

"Miss Riddell," he said, "the captain asks you to join him and Detective Somerville in his cabin right away. The chief engineer has agreed to talk to you all."

"I'll meet you at dinner, Freddie," Pauline said, with a wry expression. "You can continue talking to the passengers without asking a question while I'm away."

"It's all very well for you to make jokes about it, Polly, but it isn't funny."

Pauline didn't reply. She followed Sanchez as he quickly led the way to the captain's cabin, where Somerville, Ferguson and the chief engineer were sitting in ominous silence awaiting her arrival. The lack of conversation boded badly for their meeting, Pauline thought. Even men could usually manage some kind of small talk at times like this. She took the seat that was offered and waited for Ferguson to introduce her.

Gregor Mikailovitch stared back at the three people opposite with a calm, steady gaze.

"Gregor," Captain Ferguson began, "I want to be make it clear to you, and my two detectives here, that you are invited to talk to us about your dealings, or lack of them, with the dead man. You are not accused of anything and you shouldn't assume because we asked you here that you are."

Gregor nodded.

Before Somerville could launch into his usual deluge of accusatory questions, Pauline said, "I second the captain's statement. A question I have though is, we heard that Jose perhaps molested one of the female crew members. It's possible there were others. Had you heard this?" A surge of triumphant pleasure swept through her when she saw Somerville's surprised expression as he realized she'd learned something he hadn't.

Gregor only nodded in reply.

"Can you explain more?"

"I heard that one of the young women had been badly frightened by him. That's all."

"Did you speak, or do you know of any of the male crew members who spoke, to the dead man about this?" Pauline continued, still hoping to have Gregor open up before Somerville shut him down.

"Let's cut to the chase here," Somerville said. "Did you have a word with him and did that 'word' go too far? I mean, I can understand it if it did."

Pauline was annoyed by Somerville's intervention, but she couldn't help admiring how quickly he'd grasped the initiative on what was her evidence.

"I don't understand why you think I would kill a man because he'd made a clumsy approach to a woman," Gregor said. His expression, which had been impassive until now was becoming frosty.

Pauline stepped in. "We hear that you are something of a father-figure to the crew because of your seniority and your experience. Your wisdom, if you like."

"Do fathers kill their children if they make a mistake where you come from?"

"Of course not, but accidents happen," Somerville said.

"Why would I even want to be involved? A foolish misunderstanding between young people isn't unusual or dangerous."

"We have been led to believe it was more than just a misunderstanding," Pauline said. "We heard the young woman was seriously molested."

"That isn't what I heard," Gregor said, "and as the young man isn't here to defend himself I will continue to ask – why do you imagine any of this has anything to do with me?"

"We hear you have strict beliefs about behavior and manage the technical crew with a firm hand," Somerville said.

"Ah, I see. Believing that the crew should behave properly at all times means I murder them if they don't."

"Not at all," Pauline said. "We don't really know anyone has been murdered to be honest. We're only asked to set the company's directors' minds at rest about this awful event."

Gregor didn't reply, so Pauline continued, "We thought it possible, hearing of this serious incident you may have felt the need to confront the victim and things may have gotten out of hand."

"Let me put your mind at rest. I did speak to him about the incident. He maintained that his intentions were honorable but clumsy and the young woman was upset. These things have happened since time began. Indeed, don't you English have a nursery rhyme about it? How does it go," he paused, "Georgie Porgie, pudding and pie, kissed the girls and made them cry. Is that not right?"

"Yes," Pauline agreed, "that's how it goes but we have been led to believe it was more than just a kiss."

"I imagine it was also," Gregor said, "but without proof, there was no reason to do anything other than warn him. I saw no reason to descend to homicide." Then added, with grim humor, "At least, not at this stage."

"Where did this talk take place?" Somerville demanded.

Pauline sighed. The way he spoke really had the most annoying habit of setting people's backs up. Gregor may not have felt like killing Jose but he was becoming seriously angry with Somerville.

However, Gregor answered calmly enough. Only the martial glint in his eye suggested otherwise. "In my office, where else? These are not matters to be discussed in public."

"Are there witnesses?"

"What is it about the words 'not matters to be discussed in public' leads you to suppose there might be witnesses?"

Somerville had the grace to redden at this rebuke but continued, "You do see how this looks to an outside observer though, don't you?"

"I think a rational outside observer would be more surprised if I hadn't spoken to the young man after the incident or that I hadn't done so privately." Gregor's answers were now bordering on outright sarcasm and Pauline felt it was time to wrap this up before it deteriorated further.

"Is there anything you can tell us that might shed some light on what happened?"

"I've thought about it, as I'm sure we all have, and no, not really. It isn't against any rules for crew members to go out for fresh air, though it shouldn't be on a passenger deck. No one I've spoken to can say why Jose was where he was. It would have meant another talking to, had he not gotten himself killed."

Seeing there was no further questions, Ferguson thanked the chief engineer and Gregor left the room. The detectives turned to Ferguson.

"What do we know about your chief engineer, Captain?" Somerville asked.

"We know a lot. He's been with this ship longer than I have," Ferguson said.

Puzzled, Pauline asked, "How does an Eastern European seaman become a chief engineer on a western ship?"

"He was training as a Marine Engineer at university in Poland, where he's from. In 1956 he visited a schoolfriend who was at university in Budapest. They became embroiled in the uprising and, when the Russians stepped in to put it down, he and his friend fled to the West. Gregor finished his schooling in England and thought himself lucky because we still were the place to be for ships and shipbuilding then. It's hard to believe that now."

Ferguson paused as the realization of the speed of decline and fall once again overtook him.

He shook himself out of his reverie, and continued, "Anyway, he worked his way up the ladder, joining this ship as chief engineer when she was still sailing the Med. That was sometime in 1965, I think. Just before I arrived as a junior officer."

"Do you think he could have confronted Jose?" Somerville asked.

"No. Absolutely not. He doesn't suffer fools gladly," Ferguson paused, and then said, "but he's a good officer and he's never had a bit of bother with his crew in the twenty years I've known him. He's one of those men that people follow by example, rather than through fear."

"And you, Señor Hidalgo," Pauline said, speaking louder for the microphone, "Have you anything on those three crew members, particularly the two without alibis?"

"Nothing has come through yet," Hidalgo said. "They are just ordinary people you know, and ordinary people don't have long public records, criminal or otherwise: birth, school, marriage, children and death is about it really. There may be something different by the time we have our evening briefing."

"Then," Ferguson said, "if there's nothing else, I'll bring this meeting to a close. Thank you everyone. We will meet again after dinner and let's hope Señor Hidalgo has more for us then or tomorrow."

As they were preparing to leave, Pauline said, "Captain, would you ask Rod Chalmers to join us this evening. I think there's something to be learned there."

"I'll ask, Miss Riddell, but he's a prickly sort of fellow. He may not come."

Pauline grinned. "Prickly is the right word for Mr. Chalmers and usually I would dismiss someone so obviously suspicious from my list of suspects. Only he is evasive about his movements at the time and no one has given him an alibi, except his wife, and she's now admitted it wasn't true."

"It shall be done, Miss Riddell," Captain Ferguson said, "and we shall hope he's in an accommodating mood."

"He can be mellow after dinner and drinks," Somerville said, as Pauline and Somerville left Ferguson's cabin together and headed back toward the lounge.

Part way along the narrow corridor, Somerville stopped and, seeing he wanted to talk, Pauline did too.

"Do you believe them, Gregor and the captain, I mean?"

"Yes, I do, in the essentials."

"Ah, you aren't one hundred percent sold either then?"

"People always try to put their best foot forward. What are your reservations?" Pauline replied.

"It's too good to be true, I guess. Our chief engineer is a tough cookie and, from what I've heard, like a lot of Polish people, a staunch Catholic. He'll have old-fashioned ideas about how to deal with sex squabbles, however much he chooses to pretend he's okay with it."

"I'm a churchgoer myself, Detective, and I have old-fashioned ideas about such goings-on and yet I wouldn't advocate hurting people for lapses, but I take your point. His response was strangely tepid for something so unacceptable to him as an officer and a Catholic."

"Miss Riddell, I have a confession. At the outset I was certain this was an accident and I thought your suggestion of murder out in left field. Over the past days, I've come to think your instinct was correct. However, just for the record, even though there are a number of possibilities to this death, I still think, in the end, we'll find it was an accident."

"It's good of you to say you now see what I saw, Detective, but don't you find it compelling that this one man had so many things going against him? I doubt we'd find anyone else on this ship with a similar background of threats and horrors."

"I can't entirely agree with you there, Miss Riddell. The crew are almost all from the nearby Central and South American countries and all of them have lived with violence throughout their lives. I suspect many, if not all, share a similar history. That's even true of the passengers, who are mainly elderly people that have lived through Prohibition, the Depression, World War II, the Korean War, and so on. Take Arvin Weiss, for example."

"I've thought all that too," Pauline agreed, "but Jose is very young for such a packed history."

"Once his parents were killed, the rest I feel follows

almost naturally and doesn't necessarily point to anything bad in him. I'm almost tempted to agree with Señor Hidalgo, suicide wouldn't be beyond plausibility."

"Not implausible, I agree, but not likely in this case. He fell or was pushed backwards."

"I agree with you, not suicide, but I still feel not murder. Where does this leave us, do you think?"

"We had four viable suspects, Pedro, Rod, Arvin, and Gregor, and Pedro looks out of it for now. That leaves three. In each case, however, the opportunity appears to be there, and they have no alibis. The means is there, even though Arvin is physically weak, but none of them have a strong motive. If this is murder, and I still think it is, the reason is something we haven't discovered yet or it was something that rose quickly."

"I still favor Gregor," Somerville said. "I'm going to dive deeper into his background and movements over the past days."

"And I have changed my order of suspicion and now favor Rod, with Arvin a close second," Pauline said. "I've been researching Rod's movements these past days and got a breakthrough today, when his wife lost patience with his tiresome moodiness."

AS PAULINE and Somerville joined him for the evening briefing, Captain Ferguson said, "Mr. Chalmers has agreed to speak to us. He'll be here in ten minutes. I wanted us to have time to talk amongst ourselves before he arrived."

"And I've sent more information about the crewmen you asked about, Miss Riddell," Hidalgo said.

"I have it here," Ferguson added, handing them each two loose pages. "It isn't exciting I'm afraid."

They read and discussed the information and then what

they wanted to hear from Rod Chalmers. This was still being discussed, when an officer showed Chalmers in.

"Mr. Chalmers," Captain Ferguson said, "Thank you for coming." He gestured Rod to a seat. "Can I get you something to drink? You're a tequila man, I think."

"Sure," Rod said. "Free drinks are always welcome." His short laugh was brittle and had nothing of humor in it.

Ferguson handed him his drink. "I want to make something very clear right from the start. This isn't a police investigation and you are not being accused of anything. These two real-life detectives, in their own separate spheres, very kindly agreed to help the company confirm there was nothing sinister in the event that cost Jose Garcia his life. The police have ruled it an accident. You may have heard muttering about it being something more. We want to be sure."

Rod took a sip of his drink before saying, "What's that to do with me?"

"It seems," Pauline said, "that you were in the vicinity of the incident around the time it happened. We would like you to tell us what you heard and saw that night."

"I told you last time you asked," Rod said.

"Last time we asked," Somerville said, "you told us you weren't near where it happened. We've since learned that isn't true."

"I told you that because I heard, and saw, nothing but I knew you wouldn't believe that. It seemed easier to say I wasn't there."

"Look," Somerville said, "what happened was probably an accident brought about by unfortunate circumstances. We don't think anyone is going to be blamed for it."

"Then why bother?"

"Because there will always be a cloud over the company, ship, and crew if there isn't an understandable answer," Ferguson said.

"Whatever," Rod said. "I still can't help you."

"All we're asking is, if you and he got into a confrontation that night and he stepped back, overbalanced on the rail and fell, well, that wouldn't be murder. Just a horrible accident with no one to blame," Somerville said.

"You want me to confess to something I didn't do so you can all feel good about yourselves?" Rod said. "If, as you say, all you need is someone to say they were there and it was an accident, why don't you do it? If, as you say, no one will be blamed."

"I was in the Lounge with dozens of other people, as was Miss Riddell," Somerville said. "You are one of the very few passengers who weren't and you and Jose were seen arguing sometime earlier that afternoon."

"He wanted money from me, a tip. I said no. He didn't like my answer and said so. I threatened to inform the captain of his behavior and he became even more threatening. I walked away. After dinner, I was still seething, you might have noticed how upset I was at the meal. I went onto the forward part of the ship to smoke a cigar or two to get the bad taste out of my mouth. I didn't say anything because, from the moment I heard of his death, I knew I'd be number one suspect if anyone learned of what happened."

"Why did you think that?" Pauline asked.

"Because," Rod began angrily, and then paused and said slowly, "because it's always the Mexican that did it, isn't it? I do my best to fit in. I say 'Rod' not Rodrigo, I took my wife's family name to sound more American. I work hard to speak properly. I'm clean, tidy and have worked hard to build my fitness business but I'm still the outsider and I can't forget it. Nobody let's me."

The silence that followed this unhappy speech was deafening.

Eventually, after seeing the others had no further questions, Captain Ferguson stepped in and said, "Again, Mr. Chalmers, thank you for meeting with us and clarifying your movements that night. I think we can all see how difficult this is, and has been, for you. I don't think there's anything more we need to know."

Rod finished his drink in one steady draught, rose, nodded to them and left the cabin without another word.

"He was your first choice of suspect, Miss Riddell. What do you think now?" Captain Ferguson asked.

"I think we have to look elsewhere for our perpetrator, Captain," Pauline said.

"Then you believe him?"

"In the essentials, yes," Pauline said. "That the argument with Jose was something as trivial as a tip, no. I'm sure there's something in Mr. Chalmers' past that Jose somehow discovered but I suspect we can confirm where he was. If he was at the bow smoking, your officers on the watch that night will have seen him."

"I'll check the shift roster and we'll talk to them later," Ferguson said. "What do you think Chalmers has to hide?"

"I suspect that he isn't actually Mexican. To an English speaker, all Spanish speakers sound the same but to other Spanish speakers, they probably don't. The reverse is true, of course. Non-English speakers think we all sound the same, whereas we can say where a fellow English-speaker is from almost immediately."

"Would that be so terrible?" Somerville asked. "Not being Mexican, I mean."

"From a personal point of view, probably not, but if something important is based on him being Mexican, his immigration status to the US for instance, it may be crucial to his life going forward."

Somerville nodded. "What you say is plausible," he said.

"I think it explains his unhappiness about the whole trip.

His wife's desire to come to South America placed him in terrible jeopardy. He could be unmasked at any time," Pauline said. "The stress must have been, still must be, excruciating."

Ferguson nodded. "Is it always like this?" he asked. "Uncovering people's harmless little wrongdoings and shaming them."

"I'm afraid it is, Captain. We always learn of people's small misdeeds, their innermost doubts and fears," Somerville said. "Sometimes it's those feelings that are the cause of the crime but often, they're just why they wouldn't be honest about what happened and, in doing so, bring suspicion down upon themselves."

Pauline added. "It's often an unpleasant experience uncovering the truth," she said. "Many people have wounds that aren't fully healed."

"Well," Ferguson said, "if your principal candidate is innocent, Miss Riddell, we're left with only two. Are you ready to provide more evidence against my chief engineer, Detective?"

"Not really," Somerville said. "I've learned more about Gregor, thanks to Señor Hidalgo's good work pressing the police and others but none of it suggests he would behave as Miss Riddell thinks the possible perpetrator must have acted."

"I think a number of possibilities, Detective, not just one," Pauline interjected, annoyed at having her suspicions being narrowed down to one.

"Whatever," Somerville said, brusquely, "he is another one of the ship's company who's had an interesting life. Reading the records, I suspect his involvement in the Hungarian Uprising wasn't as accidental as he suggested. The Hungarian authorities didn't think so anyhow, after the revolt was crushed. But I think that makes him a warrior for the good guys, rather than a bully toward new recruits."

"A warrior doesn't always understand how intimidating

they are to those of us who are not warriors," Pauline said. "Jose could so easily have been scared into retreating against that gate."

"So, you still think Gregor is a suspect, Miss Riddell?" Ferguson asked.

"The reason I've never thought the chief engineer a suspect is because whoever lured Jose to that place knew what they were doing. If it was premeditated, it was murder. If it was an accident, then the chief engineer is unlikely to be the culprit. He would know he'd be suspected because he, of all people, would have, should have, known about that gate."

"So, if my bridge crew rule out Mr. Chalmers and you're both as convinced as you can be it isn't Gregor, that only leaves Arvin Weiss," Ferguson said.

Pauline said. "But we haven't entirely ruled out Pedro, Rod Chalmers or Gregor Mikailovitch. I only said the evidence isn't there to go further."

"For my part, Captain," Somerville said, "I still feel an accident is a perfectly rational explanation. The cut may have nothing to do with the event and we can't know what Jose was doing when he fell. There's no reason we know of for him to be there but that doesn't mean there wasn't a reason. The reason may be something so personal to him we've missed it."

"Such as," Ferguson asked.

"One I thought of, but it didn't check out, was he'd hidden something part way down that access ladder, drink or drugs, for example, and he was climbing down to get them when he fell backward off the ladder."

"You found nothing when you checked, you say."

"Correct. I got your maintenance guys to let me look and there was nothing and nothing was on or around the body when he was found so it didn't pan out but that just means that particular explanation wasn't right. There could be another or even others. We don't know what Jose was doing there and that's the truth of it."

"We've investigated Jose's actions and questioned those who knew him. None of them could explain it," Pauline said.

"Maybe we haven't asked the right person or asked the right question," Somerville said. "I'm ready to call this case complete now, to be honest. I think we're wasting people's time and spoiling our own, and others', vacations."

"As you might recall, I didn't want to be part of this investigation," Pauline said, "but now I am in, I'll continue to the end. I want to hear what the bridge crew have to say and then anything more that comes in about Arvin. Until we've taken the same care to eliminate him from our enquiries, we can't stop."

Somerville nodded. "I guess you're right," he said. "When can we hear from the guys on the bridge that night, Captain?"

"Before the evening is out," Ferguson said. "I'll have the officers join us and Suzanne, our hospitality manager, is also available. If you rejoin your parties, I'll have someone come find you when I have them here to talk to."

"Separately, please, Captain," Pauline said. "I'd like Suzanne's information to be as private as we can make it."

The meeting with the bridge crew, when it was held, was brief. The officer of the watch did remember a man smoking a cigar or cigarette pacing back and forth on the foredeck. While he hadn't noted the time, it was certainly around the time of the incident. He couldn't say who the man was, it was dark by that time and, even though there is low lighting on the foredeck, he was looking down from the bridge into the semi-darkness across quite a distance. All he could say for sure was a lighted cigar/cigarette moved back and forth across the deck and it was a man smoking it.

This wasn't conclusive but as no one else claimed to be

smoking on the foredeck, it looked like Rod really was in the clear.

After the bridge officer had left the cabin, Suzanne was ushered in and introduced to the detectives.

"As I asked for you to come and talk to us," Pauline said, "I'll begin. My question is a simple one. Have any of the female crew spoken to you about Jose Garcia?"

"No, no one has," Suzanne replied, puzzled. "Why?"

"You've never heard any of the women talking about him and his behavior?" Somerville asked.

"Never!"

"We thought maybe it could be a motive," Pauline said.

"He's the one dead and you're trying to blame him?" Suzanne cried.

Pauline felt she was either a very good actor or she was genuinely outraged and therefore had not heard anything against Jose.

"We have to consider all possibilities, that's all," Somerville said, stepping in to quell the manager's indignation.

Pauline felt even Somerville seemed embarrassed at having to defend them, his cheeks had flushed pink. It would be particularly galling as he'd been against this interview.

"Thank you, Suzanne," Pauline said. "You've set our minds at rest on this topic. Please don't share anything said here tonight with the others. These are difficult questions to ask and answer and no good will be served by broadcasting what has been said."

Suzanne nodded, still too upset to speak, and left the room.

"That went well, I thought," Somerville said, grinning from ear to ear.

"It had to be done," Pauline said, her mind weighing the options. Should she believe Maria's story because she didn't share it with others or disbelieve it because she hadn't shared it with others?

'Can we not distress the female staff any further, Miss Riddell?" Captain Ferguson said. "I understand your desire to be sure in this matter, but we have no reason to implicate any of them in this awful tragedy."

Pauline nodded. "I think it's clear we will learn nothing new there," she said, "so let us move on. Please send Señor Hidalgo a message urging more speed on his inquiries into Arvin Weiss," Pauline said. "He's our only remaining known suspect."

"You've ruled out the other Peruvian crew members?" Ferguson asked.

"Not entirely but nothing in the information the police provided so far would indicate a motive for murder," Pauline said.

"But we haven't ruled out manslaughter or an accident brought about by a confrontation that wasn't intended to be fatal," Somerville reminded her.

"If Señor Hidalgo sends anything new to raise any of those men in the suspect list, we can go further but at this time I'm not considering them as suspects."

"So, what you're saying, Miss Riddell, is that if we can show Arvin had nothing to do with Jose's death, you'll give up on this obstinate insistence of murder?" Somerville asked.

"If we can find nothing to indicate the likelihood of Arvin having a hand in what happened, I think we will have done enough to make the travel company feel safer, yes."

"Then let's do it," Somerville said. 'Captain, get your people working night and day on background for us, 'cos we're finding nothing here in the foreground."

"Of course, there's always the possibility of that other person, someone we haven't yet identified, being responsible," Pauline said, with only a hint of mischievousness.

"At this stage, I don't want to hear it, Miss Riddell," Somerville said, "and I'm sure Captain Ferguson doesn't either. The Ecuadorean Police had this nailed on their first day. I'm beginning to suspect you of grandstanding."

Ferguson held up his hand to draw a close to this exchange. "I just want to be sure we have nothing to fear going forward," he said. "I, and the company, don't require anything beyond that. Accident or not. We want to be sure we're not sailing with someone who is dangerous on board. Ships are confined spaces, even ones as nicely appointed as this one is, and we need to know everyone can cope with that."

"If there was wrongdoing, I want justice to be done," Pauline said. "I didn't know Jose, I have no personal interest here, but his death needs a fuller investigation than was done. I'm sorry a police detective doesn't share that opinion."

"Now listen here—" Somerville began but Ferguson intervened before he could finish.

"That's enough briefing for tonight," he said, "and squabbling won't help at this stage. We all want what's best, however we express our wish. Now, can I top up anyone's glass?"

The two detectives shook their heads.

"Then, first thing in the morning, I'll provide you with what information comes in overnight and we'll meet again tomorrow evening after dinner. Good night, and if we don't have a reason to meet first thing, enjoy Espanola Island tomorrow."

The briefing broke up and the two detectives returned to their evening entertainments. Somerville to the bar to talk sports with the men and Pauline joined Freda and Betty to listen to the nightly talk from the park naturalist telling them what to look out for on tomorrow's island.

15

ESPANOLA ISLAND, PUNTA SUAREZ

MORNING BROUGHT A NEW ISLAND AND, for Pauline, a renewed resolve. After the stretch session and sunrise, almost the best part of the day for Pauline, she and Freda went to breakfast.

"What's your plan today?" Freda asked, as they enjoyed their toast and tea in the sunshine, far away from the others.

"As we're almost sure Pedro and Rod didn't do it, I'm going to learn more about the crew and Arvin."

"We never meet the crew," Freda said, "and Arvin isn't a naturally sharing man."

"Nevertheless, I've got to try. That boy was killed and even if it wasn't murder it wasn't an innocent accident either. There was intent behind it."

"And if you don't find anything?"

"Then I go home having done what I could to right a grave wrong. I can do no more than that," Pauline said.

"I suppose," Freda said, doubtfully, "but after leading everyone to think it was murder, it will leave the people on this ship, crew and passengers alike, under a cloud. You said it was murder and there'll be no resolution. I know it sounds like I'm going back on myself, Polly, but I think you've gone too far not to finish with an answer."

"If I ask the right questions of the right people before we dock in Guayaquil again, I'll have an answer."

"I hope so," Freda said, "or people will be angry you even raised the question and kept on with it when everyone else was happy with calling it an accident."

Pauline began the renewed questioning once they reached the boat deck. Quickly realizing her queries were getting her nowhere and souring the day for everyone, Pauline rejoined Freda.

They boarded the tender in silence as it ferried them and the others of their party to the dock on the island. Calling these landing places 'docks' was too grand, Pauline thought wryly as she was being helped off the bobbing boat by a strong young sailor. There were no facilities or handrails, no gangplank, no dock offices with officials, just a flat-topped platform jutting into the sea.

They gathered around Pedro as he explained what they could expect to see and reminded them of the difficulties they would encounter on the rough paths. Looking seriously at the group, fixing the eyes of the frailest and elderly, he urged anyone who had doubts about their agility and balance to wait for the shorter hike that would begin shortly after this extended one. No one changed their mind and, with something like a shrug, he said, "We will begin."

Freda, who was anxiously watching Arvin hobble along the trail ahead of them, said quietly to Pauline, "Arvin really shouldn't have come on this excursion."

Pauline followed her gaze and saw what Freda meant. The heavy-set man was struggling with the heat and the loose rocks beneath his feet. It was difficult to know which of the two challenges was most galling to him. One hand fanned his face with a pamphlet, the map probably, while the other hand constantly reached out to nearby shrubs to steady him.

Pauline shrugged. "It will be a lesson for him," she said. "The guide said, 'strenuous walking over loose stones without shade'. Pedro gave him a clear get-out option at the start. Arvin has repeatedly told us all how much he struggles with heat and how his body has been damaged by the life he lived in Europe before emigrating to the States yet he persisted. I have no sympathy with him."

"Maybe so," Freda said, the nurse in her growing increasingly concerned, "but we'll all suffer if he has a bad accident."

Pauline was unmoved. She felt strongly that foolishness should be rewarded by its inevitable consequences.

Minutes later, Freda's worst fears came true. Arvin's ankle turned and he fell heavily, sliding down a short slope over sharp rocky outcrops.

Raul, the assistant guide, hearing Arvin's cry, stopped the group and hurried back to discover the cause. He quickly shuffled down the slope to where Arvin lay.

Freda slid down the slope behind him as quickly as she dared to the place where Arvin had fallen. "Are you okay, Arvin?" she asked.

"No, I'm not okay, you…' he cut his comment short.

"Pedro," Freda called up to where he was watching from the path, "I'm a nurse. We're going to need help here?"

Pedro quickly came down to where Freda stood.

"I'm sure you don't need my expertise to see the problem," Freda said.

"I don't. His ankle isn't right at all," Pedro said. "We can't let him walk back. I'm going to radio for help. Can you do what you can to make Mr. Weiss comfortable while I do that? I left my radio with my bag. Raul, you come and take charge of the tour while I see what can be done." He rose and both guides made their way up the incline, loose stones sliding down to bump against Freda and Arvin.

"You idiots," Arvin yelled, when a larger rock slammed into his shin.

"Lie still, Arvin," Freda said, trying to fend off the remaining stones that slid by. "I'll look at your leg if you'll let me but I'll need to take off your shoe and sock."

"No, leave it."

Freda nodded. "As you wish," she said. "There doesn't seem to be any bleeding so the skin isn't broken, everything is still inside." She smiled in what she hoped was a reassuring manner but the angle of his leg to the ankle was dramatically wrong. "Maybe it would be best if I just make you more comfortable."

She called to Pauline to bring down her bag with her spare clothes. After the drenching on their first wet landing, she'd traveled with spares.

From her bag she took a towel, bundled it, and placed it under his head.

"Is there anywhere else we need to protect," she asked.

"My side, here," Arvin said, rolling slightly so she could place a cushion there. His golf shirt was stained with blood.

"You have a scrape there, Arvin," Freda said. "Luckily, I never go anywhere without a first aid kit so let me get some antiseptic cream and a bandage on the wound before we go any further." She plunged her hand into the capacious bag and rummaged for the kit.

"Polly," Freda said, as her hand emerged from the bag, "Can you put up our umbrella and give Arvin some shade."

Pauline did as she was told, holding the sunshade so it put Arvin's sunburned face into shadow. She watched as Freda lifted the shirt up and did her best to keep her face expressionless when she saw the size of the gash in his side. She doubted Freda had any band-aids that would cover that.

"Do you have any water left, Arvin?" Freda asked.

Arvin shook his head. His eyes were closing and the color was leaving his face.

"Fortunately, we have," Freda said brightly, diving back into her bag again. "Here," she said, holding the open bottle to his lips. The water seemed to revive him and she continued, "Polly, go see what Pedro is doing. We'd all like to know help is on its way here. It's too hot to enjoy this siesta."

Pauline set off up the slope. It was hard going. The loose stones slipped under her so she seemed to slide back two feet for every one she gained. Eager hands helped up the last few feet and she was about to set off when she saw Pedro returning.

"They want to know how he is," Pedro said. "What they need to bring."

Pauline explained about the open wound and Pedro relayed that back to the ship. There was a lot of discussion in Spanish and English before a plan was confirmed. Pedro called the group together, away from Arvin, to explain.

"A team with a doctor is coming out from the ship to take Mr. Weiss back to the landing site, where a helicopter will be waiting to take him to hospital in Puerto Ayora. We will continue our tour. My assistant, Raul, will stay with Mr. Weiss until the team arrives." He held up his hand as many people were interjecting. "We must continue our walk and get back to the ship. It is very hot and many of you are not used to this heat. We will have to carry more people back if we don't go now."

The grumbling died away as people appeared to accept the wisdom of this.

"And now, Miss Riddell, I'm going to ask your sister to stay with Mr. Weiss. A trained nurse will be a valuable person to have. Raul has first aid, we all do, but this seems to be more than that."

Pauline nodded and returned with him to where Arvin lay.

Pedro outlined the plan and Freda agreed. "Of course," she said. "I'd like to stay."

"He's asleep?" Pedro asked.

"He has lost consciousness, yes," Freda said. "I've slowed down the blood loss by holding this pad against his side, but your team needs to get here quickly. More bandages would be useful."

Pedro opened his rucksack and handed over his first aid kit. Freda picked out a thick pad and a roll of dressing. "If I place this pad on the wound, instead of my spare shirt, can you tie it tightly to him with this dressing?"

Between them, they maneuvered Arvin so the dressing could be wound around his stomach and pinned in place.

As they finished, Raul joined them. "You need to go," Raul said to Pedro, "some of the older ones are beginning to droop."

"Freddie," Pauline said. She gestured to her sister to move away from the others.

When they were alone, she continued, "I know you won't like me saying this but if he wakes, ask him about the events of that night. I'm certain there's more he can tell us."

"He's a patient," Freda said, "and I'm not a torturer."

"I'm not asking you to hurt him, he's done that well enough to himself. It's just an opportunity to take his mind of his present predicament by returning to an earlier time on the trip. That's all."

"I don't believe you," Freda said, shaking her head. "Have you no compassion for anyone?"

"I have compassion for those who deserve it and I have a desire for justice for those who cry out for it," Pauline said. "You wanted to detect, now detect."

"I quit, or had you forgotten?"

"I'm only saying listen, not question, Freddie."

158

Freda strode quickly back to her patient. Pauline watched after her as she settled on the ground beside Arvin's head and adjusted the parasol to shade them both. Freda glared back at Pauline and then, shaking her head in disbelief, opened the water bottle and dribbled water onto Arvin's forehead. He stirred as the cool droplets brought him to his senses.

"What?" he mumbled.

"You have to stay awake, Arvin. The medical people will be here soon. They need you lively enough to help them."

"Rest," Arvin muttered.

"No. No rest until you're in a more comfortable spot. Now, what can we talk about to help you keep awake?" Arvin's expression became even more morose than usual. Freda continued, "What was it that attracted you to this trip, Arvin? The Darwin angle, the remoteness of the islands, the romance of the islands' history, all those pirates and whalers? What was it?"

"Darwin," Arvin mumbled.

"Me too," Freda replied, "though I'm glad we saw those giant tortoises."

"Kids stuff," Arvin muttered.

Freda laughed. "Maybe," she said. "What have you liked best so far?"

Seeing Freda was doing as a good detective should, getting the witness comfortable enough to speak freely, Pauline set off up the slope after Pedro who was seeking a higher vantage point, hoping to see the rescue team.

She rejoined the group and they set off, following the narrow trail as it snaked around the end of the island with its views out to sea. Here the vegetation was primarily low shrubs, only a few inches high, and coarse grasses. Suddenly, Pedro signaled them to halt. When they'd gathered around, he pointed to the ground, twenty yards away on the land side of the track. Large seabirds were squatted down motionless among the grasses. Even as they all began to see what he saw, a giant seabird glided down and landed with an inelegant thump beside the group,

"They're albatrosses," Pedro said. "They spend all their lives at sea, covering thousands of miles, and return here every year to this one small island to mate."

Cameras clicked and whirred as the group captured the ungainly albatross waddling across the uneven land.

"I see why they spend all their lives at sea or flying," Rod said. "I don't think I've seen anything walk that badly."

Pauline had to agree with the sentiment, it really was hopeless on land, but she remembered its huge, outstretched wings and the elegance of the bird as it glided in to land. She felt a lot could be excused just from that alone.

When the cameras stopped clicking, Pedro motioned them forward to the highlight of this excursion, a cliff down to the sea with views of the many seabirds that nested there.

"We have lost a lot of time," Pedro said to the group as they gathered around him at a lookout set back from the cliff edge, "so I will be quick outlining what you're seeing below. Then, when we're heading back to the ship, I'll answer your questions as we walk."

He spoke quickly, which meant he was hard to understand. His accent, and the age of the listeners, created confusion and the muttering among the listeners made the message even harder to hear. For Pauline, his explanation of the predatory aggression of the frigate birds directed toward the red-billed tropic birds was all she caught and that only because it accorded with her musings about the death of Jose.

Tropicbirds had long, whip-like tail feathers that are vital to their ability to maneuver underwater in their pursuit of fish and those pirates of the avian world, frigate birds, know this. They don't try to take the fish from the successful tropicbird, they attack its tail causing the tropicbird to drop the fish enabling the frigate bird, that can't dive into the sea because it has no oil in its feathers, to have a fine meal of fish.

Pauline thought this natural predatory behavior was so applicable to many human societies, groups and people. But was Jose's death the result of similar behaviors? It appeared now he wasn't really a good man but was he like a tropicbird that failed to part with the fish it had killed? And in doing so did Jose lose his ability to survive? Was his death about the worlds of politics or criminality? She smiled to herself. She could almost hear her old friend and mentor, Inspector Ramsay, saying there was little or no difference between those two ugly worlds.

She took pictures, hoping that at least one of them caught the beautiful tropicbirds as they swooped across the face of the cliffs before diving arrow-like into the sea. They entered the water leaving barely a ripple on the surface, before rising out of the water with a silver fish wriggling in their beaks. It was breathtakingly beautiful, even in its wild savagery. The attack by the huge, ugly frigate birds that followed was equally barbarous but less beautiful. She was appalled how many times the frigate birds got the fish and how hard the tropicbirds had to work just to feed themselves and probably their families somewhere on the cliff.

Finally, when she was losing hope, she saw a blue-footed booby. She'd heard so much about them and their relations, the red-footed boobies, and had yet to see one on their excursions. She was beginning to believe it was just a sailor's tale. As happens so often in life, no sooner had Pauline taken a picture of one blue-footed booby, she saw the rocks were practically littered with them. She took a second, and then a third, photo to be sure she'd have one photo to show the people at work when she got home.

Soon the group was moving again, Pedro was growing ever more anxious over his charges. They hadn't gone far when a great spout of water caught everyone's attention and they stopped again. Pedro quickly explained about the blowhole, and how the surging waves were funneled through it, before urging them back to the ship. The excited chattering and questions to Pedro passed the time quickly, which at least made the return journey seem shorter.

Back at the landing site, they discovered Arvin and the medical team had already left. Not by helicopter as Pedro had said but by a fast launch that had taken them back to the ship.

"Will he be able to continue the cruise?" one of the hikers asked Raul, who stayed behind when Arvin had left.

"I don't think so," Raul said. "His ankle is broken. I expect a government marine ambulance will be meeting us sometime tonight and he'll be transferred to hospital in the capital."

"That's sad," the woman said. "He will miss so much."

Raul nodded but said, "Perhaps not so much. There's only Gardner Bay and Cerro Hill left to see and then the voyage back to the mainland. Still, the company will find some way of helping him to complete his vacation in the future, or recompensing him, I'm sure."

"I do hope so," the woman said to a generous chorus of agreement.

Pauline wryly thought of the future dinner table guests who would be forced to listen to Arvin's continual downer diatribes and was mentally glad she wouldn't be there. She didn't wish ill of anyone but she couldn't help hoping the always sarcastic Rod would also be carried off with a similarly non-life-threatening injury.

The ride back to the ship and the champagne welcome was an annoyance for Pauline. What she wanted to know was if Arvin said anything to Freda that would help the investigation. If Arvin didn't say something indiscreet when he was in pain, he never would. Sadly, from Pauline's point of view, the guests and crew were so determined to be entertained that there was no opportunity to hear from Freda until much later.

After dinner, where the subject of Arvin's fall and removal to the mainland was discussed endlessly, Pauline and Freda walked out onto the deck to talk privately.

"You're quite the hero with our fellow passengers," Pauline said, smiling.

"Nurses, like soldiers and doctors, are heroes when we're needed – and just unseen 'backroom boys' when we're not," Freda said.

"Still, it's nice to be appreciated," Pauline said. "But to come to the point," she took one last look about before continuing, "did Arvin say anything useful?"

Freda shook her head. "No! Not really. It seems he really did go straight back to his room but," she paused, "he's sure he saw someone on deck that night when he was walking from the lounge to his cabin."

"A man or a woman?"

"He doesn't know. It was just movement in the shadows and anyway, he wears glasses. Or to be precise, he has glasses but never wears them because they make him look dorky, whatever that is."

"He didn't hear anything, or is he deaf too?"

"He said he didn't. Frankly, Polly, I don't think he would hurt anyone. He's just a frightened, lonely man whose life has been horribly shaped by the events of his childhood."

"I wasn't imagining him as an active killer but a frightened lonely man who felt threatened could easily push someone over a rail without meaning to. Didn't you notice that ornately-wrought ring on his hand? That could easily have caused the scratch under Jose's chin. No, I'm not taking Arvin off my list of suspects just yet."

"Well, he isn't coming back to the ship, Polly, so even if it was him, he's beyond your reach now."

"Not necessarily. Deduction, evidence, a process of elimination could still point to Arvin but I take your point, he is an unlikely culprit."

"What do we do now?" Freda asked, "There are no other suspects."

"We go over what we know and we think," Pauline said, but her disappointment over Arvin's apparent innocence was crushing.

It was Pedro and Rod all over again. Another dead-end and even less hope of a solution this time than last. Arvin really was the obvious candidate, not for murder, but to be the one involved. The Jose she was beginning to see better now would have found Arvin a much easier, softer target than the physically strong, and mentally aggressive, Rod, or even the kind, weak, Pedro who was despite all that, also fit and healthy. Neither of them would be an easy target to attack, even for someone as aggressive as Jose, as she now thought of him. But Arvin had fitted the bill perfectly.

16

ESPANOLA ISLAND, GARDNER BAY

ANOTHER WET LANDING, which they all now managed with the panache of Indiana Jones, and a short wade through the surf onto the colorful sand of Gardner Bay. The beach was everything the guide said it would be with sand ranging from the purest white through golden, green, red and even black, the result of lava erosion through the centuries. It was a beautiful beach with warm water, and thanks to the National Park regulations, no one was on it. Pauline and Freda tried capturing the subtle colors with their cameras, hoping they would come out when the film was processed.

Today, they'd chosen the beach-walking option to start with the possibility of snorkeling off the beach later if they chose. There was no organized hike, everyone was free to explore on their own, enjoying the silence, broken only by the soft breeze and waves on the shore.

Once they were away from the rest of the group, and after a long silence that seemed it would never end, Freda asked, "Are you still thinking it's Arvin?"

Pauline shook her head. "No," she said, "he was the most likely suspect in my mind but your kind, yet effective, interrogation rules him out as well. It's very frustrating, no one is completely cleared and yet none of them seem to have done it."

"What do the others think?"

Pauline smiled. "I thought you weren't taking an interest anymore."

"I'm just making conversation. Wandering along without a word spoken can get very tedious sometimes, Polly."

"Sorry," Pauline said. "When I'm focused on a case, I lose track of everything else. It's okay when I'm home. I have the house to myself. I forget that I'm not home sometimes."

"Honestly, Pauline. Forget Arvin. If there was ever a time when he might have given himself away, it was while he was injured. Even more so when the medics gave him painkillers. He didn't do it. Give it up."

"You're probably right," Pauline said, "but you can see how this looks to me. As you said, I pushed others to consider Jose's death a murder, and now I haven't a credible suspect left."

"It's your own fault," Freda said.

"Not entirely, Freddie, dear. As I recall, you became quite eager to have me take the case so you could help me."

Freda blushed, enough to be visible even with her sunburned face. "I was caught up in the excitement at first," she admitted.

"And now it's almost over?"

"What do you mean, almost? This is our last big island stop. Tomorrow, we have one small call into Santa Cruz and then the boat sails back to the mainland. What is there to change what we know now?"

Pauline frowned. "There's still Señor X."

"Stop being silly, Pauline. You can't just invent people when you need them."

Pauline laughed. "Says the woman with three grown children."

"That's different. We didn't invent them to pin a murder on them."

"True," Pauline agreed, "and you're right. I shall tell the others at tonight's meeting that I'm happy to call it an accident and it will all be over."

"Please do. Don't prevaricate. Be clear. Have the captain announce it on the PA. Make this whole sad story over. I want to sleep soundly in my bed. I don't want to be wedging my bedroom door shut for the rest of my life."

Pauline smiled mischievously. "But Freddie, if you had given up believing in a murderer all those days ago, why are you still jamming your cabin door shut?"

"Because you make everything so plausible," Freda replied, crossly. "I couldn't bring myself to stop."

"Then, for your sake, I will end this tonight. Now, come on, let's get back to the group before they call out the coastguard and come looking for us."

"Gladly," Freda said, "anything to get away from these insects and this infernal heat."

At the landing site, they found the others all waiting to be returned to the ship. They'd also returned to the comfort of the water's edge, where the insects were less numerous, the heat tamed by a sea breeze.

"I've decided to swim," Pauline said. "Are you coming?"

"I'm not sure we'll get our costumes dry before we have to pack," Freda said.

"We have plenty of time. If we don't swim there's nothing to do but go back to the boat," Pauline took the snorkel tube and goggles the guide offered and turned back to the beach.

Freda sighed. "I'm coming," she said, "but I'm staying near the beach. You can go out there with the others, if you wish," she pointed to the bobbing heads about three hundred yards from shore, "but I'm not."

Pauline didn't reply. When they'd undressed down to

their swimsuits, they waded into the sea, where small colorful fishes fled from their approach.

"At least it's warm here," Freda said.

"After our beach walk, I'd have preferred cooler," Pauline replied, "but it's pleasant to be out of the sun and the flies."

As they swam, a turtle rose beside them, its glassy eye examining them intently.

"They don't eat meat, do they?" Freda asked, anxiously.

"You're the one who watches Jacques Cousteau, Freddie," Pauline said. "You tell me."

"I'm sure they don't," Freda said, "but maybe we should turn around in case."

"I think it wants us to feed it," Pauline said, as the turtle kept pace.

"I'm going in," Freda said, heading back to the beach.

Pauline laughed. "You came to see the animals," she mocked her sister.

When Freda waded out of the water, Pauline knew she wasn't coming back. Placing the goggles over her face and gripping the snorkel tube between her teeth, Pauline swam on watching the turtle's effortless underwater paddling as it swam alongside.

As she approached a rocky reef, the sea life grew bigger. Small colorful fish gave way to larger even more brightly colored ones. A small ray flapped lazily along the sandy bottom below, when her shadow, and that of her turtle companion, passed over it. Cruising along the reef, she could see waving sea weeds and, she suspected, the lures of predators. As she was too big for any of them to consider lunch, they were of interest rather than fear. Her companion, however, saw the weeds as lunch and bit off pieces as they continued their journey. Pauline began to wonder if she was going to have to take the turtle home with her. It was like a stray cat or dog following her.

A small shark slithered through the water ahead of her. While she knew it wasn't dangerous, she felt it was a reminder there were things farther out that were dangerous. She waved goodbye to her turtle friend, hoping it understood this signal, and turned back toward the beach. For a moment, she thought it was going to follow. Then, with a graceful flick of its flippers, it set out toward the sea. Pauline felt she'd been abandoned.

"I wanted to let the sun dry my costume before I put my clothes back on," Freda said, when Pauline joined her on the beach.

Pauline nodded. "A few minutes in this sun will do that for us," she said.

"I'm dry already." Freda said, shaking the sand out of her Polo shirt and pulling it over her head.

"I loved the giant tortoises," Pauline remarked, "but I swear they didn't even know we were there. That turtle is now my favorite. I know it sounds crazy," she continued, "but I felt connected to it in a way I haven't with any of the other creatures here."

"You're imagining things," Freda said.

"I expect you're right," Pauline replied, placing her sun hat over her face to have a moment's respite from the sun.

"We saw lots more interesting things this morning."

"But they didn't walk a little way with me through this vale of tears, Freddie. That's the thing."

Freda shook her head and rolled her eyes. "I think you need to lie down in a dark cabin with a cold compress on your head before you go any more nuts," she said.

"Then let's go back to the ship and eat first. I'll carry my clothes and change on board."

* * *

TO PAULINE, the evening briefing with Ferguson, Hidalgo and Somerville was equally crushing. There was no new information from the mainland and when Pauline shared what Freda had learned from Arvin, there was a general almost audible sigh of relief.

"I think we've done all we need to do to satisfy the company, Miss Riddell," Captain Ferguson said.

"I agree," Somerville added. "There never was much doubt it was an accident, though we don't know the exact course of events that led to it, but Arvin Weiss was the only remaining candidate for murderer."

As this was what she'd expected to hear when she'd told them, Pauline wasn't surprised by their eagerness to wrap this up.

"The suspects we had are none of them truly cleared, gentlemen, and I can't see any plausible chain of events that would have led Jose to fall backwards over that gate so I can't altogether give this up," Pauline said, then throwing her promise to Freda overboard, continued, "I'd like us to give Señor Hidalgo and the police one more day to find something new and for us to reconsider everything we've heard before we finally call it a day."

They didn't groan out loud, Pauline was pleased to note, but she was sure they all did inwardly.

"Miss Riddell," Hidalgo's voice was always strange over the radio, "the police will not be investigating further. They have made that very clear to me. You can expect no new evidence from here."

Pauline suspected Hidalgo had heard enough and was making this story up but she couldn't blame him or any of them. It really was a waste of everyone's time. Something happened to Jose but what that was wouldn't come out of this investigation.

"And we've gone over this every night for a week now,

Miss Riddell," Somerville said. "The investigation is over. There's no compelling evidence that supports your theory and the evidence that you've highlighted has now been thoroughly investigated and, if not discredited, at least found not to be damning of anyone. I don't want to waste any more of my, or anyone else's time on it. Captain?"

"I agree, Detective. I'm sorry, Miss Riddell. Knowing of your expertise, your initial belief of murder made me persuade the company to initiate this investigation. Now, however, I don't see any need to take this further. Do you?"

Pauline hesitated. Then she said, "Very well. I hope you will announce this to the crew and passengers, Captain, for I know many people are frightened at the thought of a murderer on board. You will set many minds at rest if you do that."

"Certainly, I'll do that. I know the crew are anxious to hear the *all clear* as well. Now it is wrapped up, we need to discuss your fee, Miss Riddell."

"There will be no charge, Captain. I haven't explained either the accident or the violent death, so you and the company owe me nothing."

Captain Ferguson appeared to be about to argue but Pauline said no again and that was the end of it. The end of the official case and the detecting team but not the end of Pauline's whirlwind of thoughts.

17

AT SEA

AFTER THE BRIEFING ENDED, Pauline headed to the ship's small ecumenical chapel. She pushed open the door and stopped when she saw the priest inside. She'd hoped the room would be empty.

"Come in," the priest said, "I'm just tidying up. I'll be gone in a moment."

Pauline stepped inside and waited.

"Or did you want to speak to someone?" the priest asked.

"Only God," Pauline said. "I have a problem I'd like to discuss with him."

"Well, I'm just next door if you do want to talk," the man said. He left the chapel and Pauline took a seat near the front. The quiet was a relief after the dining and lounge areas and the general background noise of people and machinery elsewhere on the ship.

She sat for some time gazing at the plain altar and cross, that the priest had been preparing for the evening service, before lifting a thin book of prayers from the pouch of the seat in front of her. She opened it and slowly scanned the pages, hoping to find one that would give insight into the problem she was wrestling with. Because it was a book designed to meet the common elements of all the Christian faiths, none seemed to quite fit. She couldn't decide if that meant what she was looking for was in the sterner parts of the Old Testament or that what she was contemplating was just plain wrong. She closed the book and replaced it. Deciding not to wait and attend the evening service, Pauline rose, crossed herself, something she'd started doing all those years ago at the High Anglican church she'd attended with the Bertrams, and quickly left the chapel.

Back in the lounge, Freda was so involved in the card games and conversation, Pauline suspected she may not have even been missed. The moment she sat, Maria arrived to take her order.

"Good evening, Miss Riddell. Your usual English Breakfast tea and a pastry?"

"Yes, please, Maria. What pastries do we have tonight?"

"Our usual selection, Miss Riddell. I don't think there's anything new."

"Nothing new in pastries, perhaps," Pauline said, "but for me, everything seems new today. I'm sorry to say."

"I too have found new isn't always better in life," Maria said.

"Perhaps you could tell me about that," Pauline said. "Later, after your shift is finished."

"I think it will be too horrible for you," Maria said. "Where you live, horrible things don't often happen and you would be upset."

"I'm more familiar with evil than you think, Maria, and your experience may help me decide what I must do. I've a decision to make and it gives me great pain."

"Perhaps, tomorrow, Señorita. I work here late and then in the laundry."

"Tomorrow, then," Pauline said.

18

SANTA CRUZ ISLAND, CERRO DRAGON

THEIR FINAL LANDING was a dry one, for which Pauline was grateful. Trying to get everything dry in the cabin before they left the ship at Guayaquil would have been practically impossible.

As if to send them home with a vivid memory, the day was hotter than ever, the land once again rocky and broken, and the vegetation desert-like. Cerro Dragon meant 'hill of the dragons', or in this case, iguanas. The hike took them up the hill with the iguanas scuttling off the path, where they'd been sunning themselves. Pauline found the land iguanas infinitely more attractive than their marine cousins they'd been seeing on the other islands. Their coloring, which kept them camouflaged amongst the dusty, rocky ground, was less offensive to her than the ugly dark greens and reds of the sea-going iguanas.

"I wish we could have gone back to the tortoises," Freda said, as they puffed their way to the crown of the hill.

"Me too," Pauline said. As they reached the summit and the view was before them, she added, "but the hike is worth it just for this view."

"It's nice," Freda agreed, "but my vote would still be with

the tortoises. I think we can almost see them from here." She pointed to the hills farther down the coast.

Pauline nodded as she surveyed the land below them, where iguanas waddled between the short vegetation, nibbling the leaves. In places it looked like the ground was alive, there were so many.

"I was glad, relieved really, to hear the captain's announcement this morning," Freda said.

"I'm pleased you were pleased," Pauline said. Iguanas that had been scared off when they reached this spot began returning to their resting places in the sun. Not only was their sandy-colored skin more attractive, Pauline thought, their faces were too. As they strained their heads up to the sun, they seemed to smile at the warmth it gave. It wasn't quite the connection she'd felt with the turtle but it was close. Maybe she was beginning to appreciate these strange creatures just too late to enjoy them.

"You're not happy with the result, are you?" Freda said, breaking into Pauline's thoughts.

"I'm not but I'm happier with it this morning than I was when it was discussed at the briefing last night."

"What changed?"

"Overnight, with the pressure off, my mind finally settled on the truth," Pauline said.

"You don't look or sound any happier, Polly. If this is you happier, I'd hate to see you depressed. You haven't spoken a word all the way up the hill."

"I know the truth and I don't like it. We will talk to the culprit tonight and if what I hear confirms my fears, I've a terrible decision to make."

"Who is it?"

Pauline smiled. "When we hear what they say, then we can decide. Until then, you'll have to work it out for yourself."

19

AT SEA. MARIA'S STORY

"WHY ARE we meeting Maria at this time of night?" Freda asked, as they made their way along the narrow corridor servicing the cabins.

"Because I want to speak to her privately," Pauline said, "but not on my own."

"Well, I hope you're not going to tell her off or give her motherly advice," Freda said, a little crossly. They were walking more quickly than she liked and she was bumping her sides on the walls and handrails, which was painful.

"Nothing like that," Pauline said, as she opened the door to the outside deck where a stiff breeze fluttered her loose jacket. They climbed the steps up to the top deck and walked into the darkest, shadowy part.

"Hello, Maria," Pauline said.

Maria was standing at the rail, looking down to the deck below. She turned and said, "Hello."

"I'm sure you know why I asked you to meet me here," Pauline said.

"Do I?"

Pauline smiled grimly. "I have said nothing because I believe you're a good person who was driven beyond what was reasonable. Tell me what happened and why and, if I agree, it ends here tonight."

Maria met her gaze steadily, assessing this speech and its implications.

"You wish me to take the blame for this accident?" she said.

"We both know it wasn't an accident. What I want to know is, was it justice?"

Maria frowned. "Why should I trust you? You worked with that awful detective."

Pauline said, "Let me tell you what I think happened. Then you can decide if you want to let me tell anyone else." She waited to see Maria's reaction. There was none.

"Very well," Pauline said. "I'll tell you what I'm going to tell the police when we dock tomorrow. You and your boyfriend, Jose, managed to get jobs on the ship. He told you it was so you could be together. You discovered it was actually to steal from the passengers and he expected you to help him. You confronted Jose here at this spot. He was angry and you were frightened. There was a struggle, he fell. That frightened you even more and you have kept quiet since. The law may believe you, if you tell them it was an accident. Maybe you will escape jail." She paused and watched Maria, seeing the rising anger, maybe panic, in her eyes. Pauline added, "Do they have the reduced charge of manslaughter in Ecuador or will it be murder with extenuating circumstances?"

"You know nothing!"

"I think I know more than you imagine, Maria, and, as I said, if you convince me I'm right, we dock tomorrow and nothing will be said by me."

"All right. I'll tell you and it's nothing like you said."

"I know that, but the police won't."

"He was a monster," Maria cried. "He and others like him

killed my parents and molested me – isn't that what you called it? – but with sticks and guns. I can't make love. I can't have children. I have no chance of a normal life with anyone. He deserved to die for what he did."

Pauline nodded. "It was to do with the wars, I believe."

"The Shining Path, they called themselves. They are evil. There's no 'path' and nothing about them is 'shining'. God, Jesus and all the saints with the best will in their sacred beings could never forgive those creatures of darkness."

"Are you still a Catholic?" Pauline asked.

Maria shook her head. "I have heard too many in the Church excuse these demons to trust a priest anymore."

"God isn't the Church, though," Pauline said.

"The Church would have us believe otherwise," Maria said. "I believed. I attended. But neither God nor his Church were there when these animals descended on our village. I cannot forgive either of them, any more than I can forgive the monsters who massacred everyone I knew and loved."

Freda stepped forward and put her arm around Maria's shoulders to steady her for she seemed likely to fall or jump to her death.

"How did he come to be here?" Pauline asked.

Maria came out of her anguished trance and said, "I don't know. The company try so hard to screen out bad people. He told everyone he was a refugee and he got through. Then, there he was in front of me, laughing at my terror on seeing him again."

"Convince me what you say is true. Tell me what happened."

Maria frowned. "Very well," she said. "Many years ago, a couple in our small village took in a boy whose parents had been killed by Government soldiers, or at least that's what they told us. This boy, his name was not Jose, though that's the name he was going by when he arrived on this ship, was about a year older than me, maybe thirteen or fourteen. His behavior wasn't friendly and his adopted parents said it was because of what he'd seen and what happened to his parents. That seemed sensible to me and made me want to help. I wasn't the only one. Most of the children in the village tried to play with him and have him play with us but he was always angry so people began to avoid him.

"Then we got older. I got what you call a 'crush' on him. He was good looking and that moody sullen look was alluring. My parents forbade me to meet with him so I would sneak out to see him. He wasn't any better as a boyfriend than as a friend. Then one day he hit me. You won't believe it but even that didn't put me off, at least not right away.

"But it got worse and I told my parents. They were furious; you can imagine. My father talked to his adoptive parents and he was ordered to keep away from me. And I was ordered to keep away from him, though by now I understood why my parents said he wasn't bad, he was evil and I didn't need to be commanded to avoid him. I was terrified of him even then." Maria paused and then asked, "Do you believe in evil, Señorita?"

Pauline nodded. "I certainly do," she said. "I've seen too much of it to believe otherwise. There's a little of it in all of us. And a lot of it in a few of us."

"People today say there's no such thing," Maria said. "I hear them on the radio and TV, but there is. In a safe country, you forget. You imagine evil isn't there but it is. It's only waiting for the moment to strike. I can't forget, nor can I forgive."

"Go on," Pauline said.

Maria frowned. "It gets very unpleasant now," she said.

"What happened to Jose was unpleasant too," Pauline replied.

"One day, when I was in my final few weeks of school, he

disappeared. Just vanished. I have to be honest; I was happy. There were whispers that some of the men had run him out of our village. I didn't care. I just hoped he would never come back." She paused, her eyes focused on a place far away and her expression filled with pain.

After a moment, Maria continued, "Then he came back. One morning, very early, a gang of men with guns appeared out of the surrounding trees and he was among them. They said they were *Sendero Luminoso* – The Shining Path. They were Communists and they were going to make everything better for the people. But it seemed we weren't the people whose lives were to be made better. They're murderous monsters is all I know, like all of their kind."

"So, I've heard," Pauline said.

"I promise you haven't heard the full truth," Maria said. "They herded everyone into the center of the village and shot the village mayor and his wife without any warning or explanation. We children were kept apart, the boys separated from the girls. They told the adults we would be killed if they didn't give a donation to the movement."

"Women were sent to bring back all their family's money, jewelry and valuables and place it in the square. It was then I saw Jose. He was watching me and his expression was ugly. I've never seen such an expression, or at least I hadn't until that day. I saw lots then. When he was sure I was watching him, he pulled my father out of the group and shot him point-blank in the face. I screamed and ran to my father. He grabbed me and held me until my mother returned with our few valuables. Then he shot her too."

"There was uproar and some men tried to attack the revolutionaries but they were all shot. I don't think one survived. I don't know because I was dragged away by Jose and you can imagine what happened to our friends and neighbors. If you can't, know that the men were executed and the women raped, even children."

"My dear," Freda said, and stepped forward to comfort Maria but Maria stepped away.

"No," she said, "There was worse to come. Keep your comfort for yourselves, these people may well win one day and even you will not be safe."

"Go on," Pauline said.

"After he could do no more, he called others. They too were spent at this point, having had their way with all the village girls and even, they said, some boys, but at Jose's instructions, they violated me with anything to hand. They thought it was funny. How they laughed. You, Señora, are a nurse. I will show you my scars if that will convince you."

"Then what happened?" Pauline asked, her face expressionless, her voice calm and neutral.

"They grew tired and left me, expecting me to die of my wounds," Maria said, "and I was certainly desiring death, the pain was so intense, but I crawled and eventually ran. All I wanted was to be away from the village. I saw other women were running as well, all hoping to be away before the guns were turned on them."

"I hardly dared to look back because I feared they would see me and give chase. I learned later they were too busy stoning to death women and girls who hadn't tried to escape. But then my whole focus had to be on the forest ahead and the uneven ground below my feet. Once I slipped on a pool of blood and almost fell onto the body of our neighbor, Ernesto. He must have been working with his animals when the guerillas first arrived.

"The forest and safety seemed so far and I invented markers to drive myself on. They wouldn't follow me once I passed that wall, I told myself. And when that wall was passed, I invented a new marker. He definitely wouldn't follow past that broken-down truck. Then another marker; he wouldn't follow me beyond that rock. I remember thinking, beyond that rock he wouldn't even see me. Then I remember nothing."

Maria stopped and wiped the tears from her cheeks. Her face set in a furious expression, she continued…

"When I woke, I was being carried. I tried to ask what was happening. Then I woke again and I was in a tent, in a bed, and everything was white. It looked like heaven and sounded like hell, for there were people screaming, crying and moaning around me. I couldn't understand it. I felt serene, without the pain and fear I'd known. A man in white came and looked at me closely. I should have been ashamed. I wasn't ashamed. All I could feel was hate for the monsters who'd done this to me and our small community. I hated them.

"I drifted in and out of sleep and I didn't know what time or day it was. When I was awake, I still felt wonderful, far away from everything and everyone. But it seemed I wasn't as well as my serenity suggested. One day, the doctor told me I had an infection. I was to be flown to a bigger hospital in the north. I couldn't really understand why for I felt so happy, but I didn't mind. I thought being away from there would be good.

"But it wasn't good. My insides hurt. My head hurt. Being carried to the plane wasn't comfortable and the buffeting in the plane during the flight was worse. By the time I was carried off and back to a new bed, I couldn't stop weeping. The following days were a blur. The following weeks, mercifully better. One day the pain in my stomach and groin was bearable, I could walk with help. Soon after I could walk unaided, and not long after that I could hardly remember the pain. Only the scars remained to remind me. That, and the bad dreams.

"My wounds, however, turned out to be in my favor. I was accepted as a refugee to Ecuador and I gratefully accepted. I hoped that I would never again see my country or my fellow citizens for if I did I wasn't sure I wouldn't try to kill them. It was a relief when I flew out to my new home in Quito.

"My relief, my pleasure, however, drained away as the days became weeks and then months. I knew no one and work was hard to come by. I had no skills that would pay as well as I needed for the medicines I have to take. All that I could find were cleaning jobs in hotels and they were dreary. Then I saw an advertisement for cleaners on a cruise ship and I applied. Sunshine and warmth were what I craved. Quito's weather, swinging between biting cold and then draining heat made me feel suicidal. And the pay was better, much better on the ship. A month later, just two weeks ago, I joined the ship at Guayaquil as it prepared to take visitors from Europe and North America to the Galapagos Islands."

"That's when it happened?" Pauline said.

Maria nodded.

"There was a staff meeting the day before, where we went over our training lessons. Others on the ship had worked for other cruise lines. I was one of the few new staff and didn't know anyone so I was alone in the group as we walked down the corridor back to our quarters. We passed through an open area where a group of men in coveralls were talking amongst themselves, seemingly innocent but I suspected they were hanging about to check out the girls.

"Suddenly, I found my sleeve being tugged and I turned to face the man who held it. Even with the beard and moustache, I recognized him instantly. My whole body froze and I couldn't breathe.

"'You made it too,' he said, in a conversational tone like

we were friends meeting again after escaping a disaster. 'We must talk.'

"'Sadly, so did you, I said. We will not talk or meet. Get away from me.'

"'Go on deck seven, at the port side smoking area. I'll meet you there,' he told me.

"'I will not meet you anywhere and if you come near me again, I will tell the ship's security and they will inform the police," I said. 'Your only hope for a future outside jail is to leave me alone and leave this ship at the end of the voyage.'

"He let my arm go. 'I'm a refugee also. My story is as good as yours. Deck seven, I'll meet you there.'

"I returned to my room. I was shaking so hard I could hardly walk, my mind reeled at the shock. I slumped on the bed and tried to plan. Would security even believe me? Then my dismay turned to rage, and I knew what I was going to do. If he'd left me alone, he would have been safe. He wasn't going to do that, so I would take my revenge. It was simple justice, in my mind."

Pauline watched her carefully as she spoke, unhappy at the choice before her. If Maria's story was true, then it was a just ending to Jose's violent, cruel life. But was her story true? She should ask Freda to examine Maria but, if her story was true, that would be an additional cruelty practiced upon a woman who had suffered, and continued to suffer, more than anyone should have to. "Nevertheless," Pauline said, "it is not for private citizens to execute others. You should have alerted the captain and had Jose arrested."

"Perhaps, if I was someone from another country, another world, who had stumbled upon Jose's secret, that's what I would have done. But I am not that neutral observer from another world. I was terrified and at the same time consumed with rage. He still had the chance to leave me alone. That's all I asked. It wasn't too much to ask, was it?"

Pauline didn't reply.

Maria continued, "I took a steak knife from the crew's dining room and met him on deck seven, as he'd demanded but not the place he'd chosen. I waited in a dark corner, this dark corner, where no one would see him with me. I didn't want anyone to think I would be with such a creature. And I had a plan.

"Maybe my choice of a dark corner was a mistake. Maybe it led him to think I was giving in to him. I don't know. He grabbed my arms and pulled me to him. I thrust the knife point under his chin. He stepped back. The gate swayed and moved and he toppled. He let go of me and tried to grab the railings, but he was too slow. He seemed to hang in the air forever, his behind resting on the wobbly rail, and then slowly, too slowly to my eyes, slid off and down." She paused, her expression filled with horror and her eyes focused far away.

"But you knew the place you'd chosen was dangerous, didn't you? How did you know that?"

"Yes, I knew. During the orientation to the ship, the staff were taken on a tour. It was hot and sunny and on deck seven, where there's nothing above, many of us gathered in this corner where there was a little shade from the superstructure. Those of us at the back of the group, leaned against the railing. One of the girls leaned against the gate and it moved. Her neighbors grabbed her before she fell. We giggled quietly for we didn't want the officer giving the talk to think we weren't listening. It was nothing. Silliness."

Maria's attention once again drifted away to the times before and she seemed lost to her present danger.

"And then?" Pauline asked sharply, to bring Maria out of her trance.

"When he said meet on deck seven, it came back to me. I

knew that God, or maybe just natural justice, had created this chance for me to make him pay for his crimes."

"Go on. What happened when he fell?"

"I looked over the rail when I heard him hit the deck below. He was lying still but I didn't know if he was just unconscious or really dead. I ran quickly down the steps to where he lay. He was dead. I'd been terrified of him when he was alive and now I found I was equally terrified of him dead. Everything would come out and they would say I murdered him. No one was about. I heard no one coming. I ran back to my room and threw the knife overboard on the way."

"How did you know he was dead?" Freda asked.

Maria stared at her as if she were mad. "I saw so many dead people on the day he and his friends mutilated me. He was dead. I was only sorry I had killed him, for it put my own life, so recently regained, back in peril. I didn't think he was dead because I wished it but because I could see it."

"You may not have killed him directly but you were responsible for his death," Pauline said. "You told me you had been a believer once, does your conscience not give you pain?"

"When he grabbed me that first day on the ship, my faith had been returning slowly and then he was standing in front of me, laughing at my terror. I thought, why would any just God do this to a follower who had suffered as I had? I don't know the answer to that. A priest would say the answer might lie beyond this life. But I know in this life I have suffered beyond what anyone should have to and I wanted my life back. You perhaps think I should suffer more. Well, I have told you the truth. I place myself, and my future, in your hands, Señorita Riddell. Choose wisely."

Maria turned abruptly and walked away, leaving Pauline and Freda to gaze after her.

"Pauline," Freda said, at last, "you can't."

"I believe in the law, Freda. Without it, we return to a world where the strong prey on the weak and might is always right. Sometimes, as we struggle to maintain our laws, things will be other than what we wish. This is one of those times."

"I will not give evidence against Maria," Freda said.

"Have you heard Jose's side of the story?"

"No, but—"

"Then how do you know what we heard is true or, if essentially true, doesn't have a different explanation?"

"I could ask to see her wounds," Freda said.

"Do only the innocent have wounds?"

"No, but—"

"It's not for us to decide. It's for a court."

"I'm going to bed," Freda said icily, and stalked away.

20

ECUADOR AND TORONTO

CAPTAIN FERGUSON HELD the cabin door as Pauline walked into his room.

"Good morning," she said to Ferguson and Somerville. "Did you start without me?"

Ferguson shook his head. "Not at all, Miss Riddell, we couldn't. You were the one who wanted more time," he said. "We've been discussing nothing more than the cruise and the islands. But, now you're here, and you both have very little time before disembarking, perhaps you, Miss Riddell and you, Detective Somerville, can give me any last minute, or final, thoughts. Can I tell the owners that all is well?"

Somerville looked at Pauline sternly before saying, "Miss Riddell rightly drew our attention to an injury on the dead man's chin and suggested that this event was a murder and not an accident. I've looked at all the evidence, interviewed dozens of people. We've had information radioed and faxed in from the Peruvian and Ecuadorian Police departments and I can see no evidence of any wrongdoing. I have to conclude the scratch under the dead man's chin has no bearing on his fall and death, however it might look to Miss Riddell. The Ecuadorian Police examined the scene the morning after the incident. They saw no reason to call it murder either."

Captain Ferguson turned his attention to Pauline.

Pauline waited a moment to get a grip on herself before she said, "And I have no hard evidence to dispute Detective Somerville's or the Ecuadorian Police's conclusion, Captain. The company should not be concerned about this incident, beyond replacing that loose gate and I know you've already done that."

"Thank you, both of you. You've taken a load off my mind. The thought we had a murderer on board who might strike again at any moment has been a concern to me throughout the voyage, as you may imagine."

"There never was a murderer," Somerville said. For a moment it seemed he would go on but he left it at that.

"I think you can be sure there will not be another incident of this kind on the ship," Pauline said. "Now, I will take your leave for I've still some final packing to finish before I put my bags out. Thank you for a wonderful cruise, Captain, and for taking my concerns seriously." She held out her hand. They shook hands briefly and Pauline turned to detective Somerville.

"Mr. Somerville," she held out her hand, "it was nice to meet you. I do hope you have a good trip home."

With that, she left the cabin and strode quickly down the corridor to her room. She stopped. Her mind made up, she headed back toward the lounge where snacks had been laid out for those waiting to leave the ship.

"Maria," Pauline said, as the server emerged from the kitchen area with a tray of croissants.

Maria placed the tray on a table and removed the empty one she was replacing. She walked to where Pauline was waiting.

"Yes?" She asked.

Pauline hesitated. "I can't approve of what you did," she said, "but I will take your secret with me today. I wish you all the happiness you can have in your life. Goodbye. God bless."

With that, she turned abruptly and walked away leaving Maria gazing sadly at her retreating figure.

"Well?" Freda demanded, when she was allowed into Pauline's cabin.

"Well, what?"

"As half this detective team I want to know what you told the captain."

"You quit the team, if you remember, but I will tell what I told him. He need have no fears arising from this incident."

"You didn't tell him about Maria?"

"It goes against everything I hold dear," Pauline said, "but I think this may be the one instance I've ever met where justice has been served without the law's involvement. Maria has justice and, I believe, in his own way, so has Jose, or whatever his name was. Now let's go. I never want to see this ship or these people again."

"Why? What have they done?"

"Nothing," Pauline said. "It's what I've done that makes it impossible for me to meet them again."

"You're too hard on yourself, Polly. No one would have handed Maria over to the police."

"I'm not *no one* and I believe in the law and its importance for the safety of us all. You're happy at my decision; I'm glad of that. But, I am not and I will live with what I've done forever."

* * *

"WHAT MADE you think it was Maria, Polly?" Freda asked, as they sat on their hotel's terrace in the bright sunshine overlooking one of Quito's quieter parks.

It was the first time they'd been alone that day. The disembarkation had been orderly but busy with people and the leave-taking noisy. The coach ride back to Quito had been quieter, everyone feeling that letdown that comes at the end of every trip. The coach dropped each group at their hotels and the goodbyes now were weary ones. Pauline and Freda were among the last to be dropped off but there were still too many passengers to talk safely.

"The first moment was when you asked her if she knew Jose from before and she didn't answer."

"She did," Freda said.

"No, she didn't. She shook her head. A person like Maria couldn't actually say a lie but she could shake her head. Many people are like that."

"But she told us about what he'd done."

"Yes. She had to or we would have been suspicious of her agitation over the questions."

"And that was it?"

"It was the first suspicion I had we were wrong about Jose. Then Pedro said Jose pretended machismo but was not a manly man and I thought of the people Jose had quarrels with, Arvin, Pedro, Rod, and Maria."

"But Arvin quarreled with Jose, not the other way around."

'Possibly but Arvin didn't wear his glasses. What if Jose *had* been stealing his bag from his room and Arvin had been wrongly persuaded it was all a mistake?"

"But Pedro and Rod? How could they be involved?"

"Jose was a man who sniffed out weaknesses and attacked them without mercy. I'm sure he heard Rod speaking Spanish to one of the crew, heard the discrepancy and saw an opportunity for blackmail. And poor Pedro was even more at risk. I'm sure Jose knew Pedro's weakness from long before and again saw the opportunity for gain."

"But if Maria had gone to the captain, he'd have been found out," Freda said.

"Jose had only to go to the captain first and say it was Maria who'd led the guerillas to the village that day. We may have believed Maria over him but it would be hard to prove otherwise. He wasn't a 'manly man', to use Pedro's words, but he was cruel and audacious. I suspect in the end, it would be Maria who broke first."

"But none of these things say Maria did it," Freda said.

"On their own, each one was as unproveable as the evidence against our suspects in Jose's death. But together, I saw a pattern, not a series of random chances, and people – people with weaknesses, ripe for exploitation. From that, I saw a different Jose."

"I still don't see why Maria and not the others."

"Do you remember the first time we met Maria?"

"Not really."

"I noticed and mentioned her name badge said she was from Peru. She was quick to say she now lived in Ecuador and added 'among good people'. I thought it an odd thing to say. I live in Canada now but I don't think Britons are not 'good people' and Canadians are better."

"It was just her way of saying how much she liked her new home," Freda protested.

"I thought that too, until everything we thought we knew began to shift."

"But you were still guessing he'd done something to Maria, personally I mean."

"And if it was only what I suspected I would have given my suspicions to the police. It was the horror of what she told us and her offer to show her scars to prove it that, in the end, decided me."

"What if Maria had denied all of it."

"Then my decision would have been a much harder one to make, for I was sure I was right."

Freda shuddered, though the evening was warm.

"I like what you do even less, now," she said.

"This case has opened my eyes too," Pauline said. "Now, I'm going to have an early night. It's been a long day and I didn't sleep at all last night."

"With your conscience, I'm surprised you ever sleep at all," Freda said, rising from her chair and following her sister into the hotel.

Pauline didn't reply. In her mind, she saw Jose letting go of Maria's arms and trying to escape the knife under his chin while reaching for the solid railing. Could he have been forced far enough back by the knife to lose his balance? Or when he tottered on the gate, hanging between this world and the next, did Maria flip his legs up and achieve her justice. On balance, pardoning the pun, Pauline thought it didn't matter to her decision. She had no doubt that, had Jose lived, Maria would not have survived that night. He couldn't risk her staying silent for the whole voyage.

*　*　*

A WEEK later Pauline said goodbye to Freda at Toronto Pearson Airport.

"You will come home next year, won't you, Polly?"

Pauline nodded. "Of course, and we'll have a family reunion at the Raven Hall Hotel. You'll organize it. Get everyone together."

"I'd like that," Freda said. "We don't see the boys as much these days. Not since mum died."

"Mothers keep families together, it's true."

The line at the departure gate had gone and the staff were giving Freda 'that look'.

"I have to go," she said. "I don't like leaving you here all alone, Polly. Look after yourself."

"I'm not alone," Pauline said. "I have colleagues at work and new friends in the neighborhood. And if I get lonely, I can call you on the phone at any time or be home with you all in a few short hours, thanks to the magic of jet travel. Have a great flight, Freddie."

Pauline watched Freda exit down the tunnel, waving as she went, before making her own way back to her car. Her sister's words had hit a nerve. One that had been jangling since that last morning on the ship. Her life, her real life, had been solving the puzzles that had come her way. Her job had always felt secondary to that. Helping people to get justice had been her passion and her whole reason to be. And now it was gone. Murdered by her betrayal of her own principles. What right did she have to hold others to laws that she was prepared to flout when the occasion arose?

She sat in the car staring at the rows of vehicles parked in the garage. Surely, she thought, her self-disgust would pass soon and she could begin investigating again? She started the engine and drove out into the sunlight. She felt she'd betrayed herself and she must never investigate again for she could not be sure she wouldn't choose to follow her feelings instead of the rule of law. Once you start down that path, it becomes simply vigilantism. That life, it seemed, which had sustained her through the long, lonely years as Stephen's 'widow', felt over.

It was strange to be thinking of Stephen again so vividly. It was this case and how it felt like that first one. A sudden faint smile came to her lips when she remembered the letter she'd received at the end of that first case, asking for her help. In a way that's how it all began. Not with Marjorie's murder but with the letter from Mrs. Elliott. If she'd never received that letter when she did, she would never have become 'Miss Riddell' and all that entailed.

Her smile deepened. Today's mail hadn't arrived before she'd driven Freda to the airport. Could history and the mail service repeat itself? For the first time in days, she felt herself awakening, hope rising and the belief she still had a role to play returning. There would be a letter, she just knew it.

The End
(of this book anyway)

POLITE REQUEST

Thank you for reading my book. If you love this book, please, please don't forget to leave a review on Amazon! Every review matters and it matters a lot for independent authors!

I'll make it super-easy to do that on Amazon by placing the link here:

It's Murder, On a Galapagos Cruise

And THANK YOU now and forever if you do:-)

BONUS CONTENT

Here's an excerpt from the next book in my cozy mystery series:

Chapter 1: Newcastle-upon-Tyne, England, December 1953

Pauline stared at the letter in her hand, hardly daring to believe it possible. Only minutes ago, she'd been wondering how she could change her life to make something more exciting of it and here it was. A letter from a woman, Mrs. Elliott, who wanted her help and all because she'd been mentioned in the newspapers as having solved a murder when the police had given up. If it wasn't for the letter, which she could clearly see and feel in her hand, she'd have thought herself in a dream. A dream from which she'd wake and be disappointed.

She held up the letter so she could see it better in the light streaming through the window from the nearby streetlight. The words seemed to float on the page, drawing her in.

'Dear Miss Riddell,

I saw the article in the Herald yesterday and your amazing success in unmasking those killers. I have a puzzle the police won't look at, but somebody should. I thought, hoped, you might like to. I can't pay very much, I'm not rich but it may interest you. It's not a serious thing like murder but it is puzzling, and it worries me. Sorry if you think I'm rambling. I just can't get it out of my mind. Maybe it would be better if I explained a little, then you'd see.

First, you should know I live in an old house on the outskirts of Mitford. It's very quiet, or at least it was. Recently, I've heard noises, particularly at night. I have a good security alarm system and I lock up carefully, so I don't believe I'm in any danger. However, something is going on.

A week ago, I was crossing a stream on my daily walk by a bridge I've used every day, twice a day, since I retired. There's never been any trouble. On this occasion, the bridge had come loose and it tipped me into the stream. Fortunately, though I'm old, I'm not frail and while I'm cut and bruised, I'm not seriously hurt. But I could have been. I showed the bridge to the police and told them about the noises, but our local policeman man says the bridge is old and the bad weather has driven a lot of animals to find shelter in and around houses. What he said is true, but it doesn't explain it. I've lived in this house nearly forty years now and I know every creak – and so does Jem, my dog.

I have more to tell you, however, you may not be interested. If you are, please phone me at this number and I'll explain more fully.

Yours Sincerely,
Doris Elliott

Pauline put down the letter and walked to the window, where the cold December night was lit by the lights of houses opposite and a nearby streetlamp. She told herself she wanted to think about this invitation. Should she raise this woman's hopes and then dash them because she couldn't provide answers or because the answers were as ordinary as the local policeman said? She shook herself. What on earth was she thinking of? Of course, she'd phone and accept the cry for help. After all, it wasn't just Mrs. Elliott who needed her to use her gifts, she needed to use them as well. The new life she'd wondered about was stretching out before her. There could be no question about turning away. She glanced at her watch. It was too late to call now. She'd phone Mrs. Elliott after church in the morning.

If this excerpt has whetted your appetite for more, you can now pre-order Then There Were ... Two Murders?

Or you can read more of Miss Riddell's adventures right away:

Starting with the first published book in the Miss Riddell Cozy Mystery series, In the Beginning, There Was a Murder

Or the third published book of the series, A Murder for Christmas

Or the fourth published book of the series, Miss Riddell and the Heiress

MORE OF MY BOOKS

You can find more books by P.C. James and Paul James here:

P.C. James Author Page: https://www.amazon.com/P.-C.-James/e/B08VTN7Z8Y

Paul James Author Page: https://www.amazon.com/-/e/B01DFGG2U2

GoodReads: https://www.goodreads.com/author/show/20856827.P_C_James

NEWSLETTER

To be kept up-to-date on everything in the world of Miss Riddell Cozy Mysteries, sign up to my Newsletter here.

For my family. The inspiration they provide and the time they allow me for imagining and typing makes everything possible.
I'd also like to thank my editors, illustrator and the many others who have helped with this book. You know who you are.

Copyright © 2021 by P.C. James All rights reserved.

No part of this book may be reproduced in any form or by any electronic or mechanical means, including information storage and retrieval systems, without written permission from the author, except for the use of brief quotations in a book review.

It's Murder, on a Galapagos Cruise© Copyright <> PC James Copyright notice: All rights reserved under the International and Pan-American Copyright Conventions. No part of this book may be reproduced or transmitted in any form or by any means, electronic or mechanical, including photocopying and recording, or by any information storage and retrieval system, without permission in writing from publisher. This is a work of fiction. Names, places, characters, and incidents are either the product of the author's imagination or are used fictitiously, and any resemblance to any actual persons, living or dead, organizations, events, or locales is entirely coincidental. Warning: the unauthorized reproduction or distribution of this copyrighted work is illegal. Criminal copyright infringement, including infringement without monetary gain, is investigated by the FBI and is punishable by up to 5 years in prison and a fine of $250,000.

EVEN MORE INFORMATION

Email: pcjames2523@gmail.com
Twitter: https://twitter.com/pauljames953
Facebook: https://www.facebook.com/pauljamesauthor
Facebook: https://www.facebook.com/PCJamesAuthor/MissRiddellCozyMysteries

ABOUT THE AUTHOR

I've always loved mysteries, especially those involving Agatha Christie's Miss Marple. Perhaps because Miss Marple reminded me of my aunts when I was growing up. But Christie never told us much about Miss Marple's earlier life. When writing my own elderly super-sleuth series, I will trace her career from the start. As you'll see, if you follow the Miss Riddell Cozy Mysteries over the coming years.

However, this is my Bio, not Miss Riddell's, so here goes with all you need to know about me: After retiring, I became a writer and, as a writer, I spend much of my day staring at the computer screen hoping inspiration will strike. I'm pleased to say, it generally does — eventually. For the rest, you'll find me running, cycling, walking, and taking wildlife photos wherever and whenever I can. My cozy mystery series begins in northern England because that was my home growing up and that's also the home of so many great cozy mysteries. Stay with me though because Miss Riddell loves to travel as much as I do and the stories will take us to many different places around the world.

facebook.com/PCJamesAuthor
twitter.com/pauljames953

Printed in Great Britain
by Amazon